Also by Jack Higgins

JACK HIGGINS

The Graveyard Shift

HARPER

Harper
An imprint of HarperCollins*Publishers*
77–85 Fulham Palace Road,
Hammersmith, London W6 8JB

www.harpercollins.co.uk

This paperback edition 2012
1

First published in Great Britain by John Long 1965

A catalogue record for this book is
available from the British Library

ISBN: 978-0-00-723492-9

Set in Sabon LT Std by Palimpsest Book Production Limited,
Falkirk, Stirlingshire

Printed and bound in Great Britain by
Clays Ltd, St Ives plc

PUBLISHER'S NOTE

THE GRAVEYARD SHIFT was first published in the UK by John Long in 1965. It was later published in paperback by Penguin but has been out of print for several years.

In 2012, it seemed to the author and his publishers that it was a pity to leave such a gripping story languishing on his shelves. So we are delighted to be able to bring back THE GRAVEYARD SHIFT for the pleasure of the vast majority of us who never had a chance to read the earlier editions.

As always – for Amy

When the times change, all men change with them. So many of both the friends and critics of the police talk as if police constables were not men.

—WITNESS, ROYAL COMMISSION ON
POLICE POWERS

To the ordinary soldier, the battle is his own small part of the front.

—GENERAL GRANT

Central Index   POLICE DEPARTMENT   Form No. 272
30/3B/112   File No.
SERVING OFFICER'S RECORD CARD   372/1/6

NAME: MILLER Nicholas Charles   NUMBER 982
ADDRESS: 'Four Winds,' Fairview Avenue
DATE OF BIRTH: 27th July, 1939
AGE ON JOINING DEPARTMENT: 21
OCCUPATION ON JOINING DEPARTMENT: Student
EDUCATION: Foundation Scholar at Archbishop Holden's
              Grammar School
         Open Exhibition to London University 1956
        London School of Economics
EDUCATIONAL ATTAINMENT: Bachelor of Law with
                             Second Class Honours,
                             University of London,
                             1959
SERVICE RECORD: Joined Department, 1/2/60
                  Passed out District Training centre,
                     1/5/60
                  Certified as passing probationary year
                     satisfactorily, 1/2/61
                  Appointed to Central Division, 3/3/61
                  Appointed Detective Constable and
                     transferred to 'E' Div. on 2/1/63
                     (See File National Bank Ltd.,
                     21/12/62)
                  Need to sit promotion exam waived by
                     Watch Committee and put forward
                     for place at Bramshill, 2/12/63 (See
                     File Dale-Emmett Ltd., 3/10/63)
                  Completed Special Course Bramshill
                     with Distinction and promoted sub-
                     stantive Detective Sergeant, Central
                     Division, effective 1/1/65
COMMENDATIONS: 1/8/60 See File 2/B/321/Jones R.
                 5/3/61 See File 2/C/143/Rogers R. T.

4/10/61 See File 8/D/129/Messrs.
Longley Ltd.
5/6/62 See File 9/E/725/Ali Hamid
21/12/62 See File 11/D/832/National
Bank Ltd.
3/10/63 See File 13/C/172/Dale-
Emmett Ltd.

CONFIDENTIAL ASSESSMENT: A highly intelligent officer
with a genuine capacity for police work who possesses
potential leadership qualities of a high order. Greatest fault, a
tendency to work on his own. Tends to unorthodoxy in
methods. It should be noted that this officer is a judo brown
belt and an exponent of the art of karate, a Japanese mode of
self-defence by which it is possible to kill an opponent with the
bare hands. The undesirability of using such methods in the
execution of his duty has been pointed out to this officer.

1

Fog drifted up from the Thames, pushed by an early morning wind, yellow and menacing, wrapping the city in its yellow shroud, and when the duty officer at Wandsworth opened the judas gate and motioned the half dozen waiting men through, they stepped into an alien world.

Ben Garvald was last in line, a big, dangerous-looking man, massive shoulders swelling under the cheap raincoat. He hesitated, pulling up his collar, and the duty officer gave him a quick push.

'Don't want to leave us, eh?'

Garvald turned and looked at him calmly.

'What do you think, you pig?'

The officer took an involuntary step back and flushed. 'I think you always did have too much bloody lip, Garvald. Now get moving.'

Garvald stepped outside and the gate clicked into place with a finality that was strangely comforting.

He started to walk down towards the main road, passing a line of parked cars and the man behind the wheel of the old blue van on the end turned to his companion and nodded.

Garvald paused on the corner, watching the early morning traffic move in a slow line through the fog, judged his moment and crossed quickly to the small café on the other side.

Two of the others were there before him, standing at the counter while a washed-out blonde with sleep in her eyes stood at the urn and made fresh tea in a metal pot.

Garvald sat on a stool and waited, looking out through the window. After a while, the blue van cut across the line of traffic through the fog and pulled in at the kerb. Two men got out and entered the café. One of them was small and badly in need of a shave. The other was at least six feet tall with a hard, rawboned face and big hands.

He leaned against the counter and when the girl turned to Garvald from serving the others, cut in quickly in a soft Irish voice:

'Two teas, me dear.'

He challenged Garvald to say something, a slight, mocking smile on his mouth, arrogantly sure of himself. The big man refused to be drawn and looked into the fog again as rain spattered against the window.

The Irishman paid for his teas and joined his

companion, at a corner table and the small man glanced furtively across at Garvald.

'What do you think, Terry?'

'Maybe he was hot stuff about a thousand years ago, but they've squeezed him dry in there.' The Irishman grinned. 'This is going to be the softest touch we've had in a long, long time.'

The girl behind the counter yawned as she filled a cup for Garvald and watched him out of the corner of her eye. She was used to men like him. Almost every morning someone crossed the road from the place opposite and they all had the same look. But there was something different about this one. Something she couldn't quite put her finger on.

She pushed the cup of tea across and brushed the long hair back from her face. 'Anything else?'

'What have you got?'

His eyes were as grey as woodsmoke on an autumn day and there was strength there, a restless, animal force that was almost physical and she was aware of her body reacting to it.

'At this time in the morning? You're all the same, you men.'

'What do you expect? It's been a long time.'

He pushed a coin across the counter. 'Give me a packet of fags. Not tipped. I want to taste them.'

He lit a cigarette and offered the girl one, the two men in the corner watching him in the mirror. Garvald ignored them and gave her a light.

'Been up there long, then?' she said, blowing out smoke expertly.

'Long enough.' He looked out of the window. 'I expect I'll find a few changes.'

'Everything's changed these days,' she agreed.

Garvald grinned and when he reached out, running his fingers through her hair, she was suddenly breathless. 'Some things stay the same.'

And then she was afraid and her mouth turned dry and she seemed utterly helpless, caught in some inexorable current. He leaned across the counter quickly and kissed her full on the mouth.

'See you some time.'

He slid off the stool and with incredible speed for such a big man, was out through the door and moving away.

The two men in the corner went after him fast, but when they reached the pavement, he had already disappeared into the fog. The Irishman ran forward, and a moment later caught sight of Garvald walking briskly along. He turned a corner into a narrow side street and the Irishman grinned and nudged the small man with his elbow.

'He's really asking for it, this one.'

They turned the corner and walked along the uneven pavement between decaying Victorian houses fringed with iron railings. The Irishman paused, pulling the other man to a halt, and listened, but the only sound was the roar of the early morning traffic from the main road, strangely muted by the fog.

A frown creased his face and he took an anxious step forward. Behind him, Garvald moved up the steps from the area in which he had been waiting, swung the small man round and raised a knee into his groin.

He sagged to the pavement with a gasp of agony and the Irishman turned round. Garvald stood on the other side of the writhing body, hands in the pockets of his raincoat, a slight smile on his face.

'Looking for somebody?'

The Irishman moved in fast, great hands reaching out to destroy, but they only fastened on thin air and his feet were kicked expertly from beneath him.

He thudded against the wet flagstones and scrambled to his feet cursing. In the same moment, Garvald seized his right wrist with both hands, twisting it round and up, locking the man's shoulder as in a vice.

The Irishman gave a cry of agony as the muscle started to tear. Still keeping that terrible hold in position, Garvald ran him head-first into the railings.

The small man was being sick into the gutter and now he got to his feet and leaned against the railings, an expression of horror on his face.

Garvald stepped over the Irishman and moved a little closer and the small man felt such fear as he had never known before move inside him.

'For Christ's sake, no! Leave me alone!' he gabbled.

'That's better,' Garvald said. 'That's a lot better. Who sicked you on to me?'

'A bloke called Rosco – Sam Rosco. He and Terry did some bird together at the Ville a couple of years back. He wrote to Terry last week from this dump up North where he lives. Said you were bad news. That nobody wanted you back.'

'And you were supposed to convince me?' Garvald said pleasantly. 'How much was it worth to pass the message along?'

The small man moistened his lips. 'A century – between us,' he added hastily.

Garvald dropped to one knee beside the Irishman and turned him over, whistling a strangely sad little tune in a minor key as he searched him. He located a wallet and took out a wad of five-pound notes.

'This it?'

'That's right. Terry hadn't divvied-up yet.'

Garvald counted the money quickly, then slipped it into his inside breast pocket. 'Now that's what I call a very satisfying morning's work.'

The small man crouched beside the Irishman. He touched his face gingerly and recoiled in alarm. 'Holy Mother, you've smashed his jaw.'

'You'd better find him a doctor then, hadn't you?' Garvald said and turned away.

He vanished into the fog and the sound of his whistling hung on the air for a moment, then faded eerily. The small man stayed there, crouched beside the Irishman, the rain soaking through the shoulders of his cheap coat.

It was the tune – that damned tune.

He couldn't seem to get the sound of it out of his head and for some reason he could never satisfactorily explain afterwards, he started to cry, helplessly like a small child.

2

And then there was the night with a cold east wind that swept in all the way from the North Sea like a knife in the back, probing the alleys of the northern city, whistling along the narrow canyons that divided the towering blocks of flats that were the new housing developments. And when the rain came, it was the cold, stinging rain of winter that rattled the windows like lead shot.

Jean Fleming sat on a hard wooden chair in the main CID office at Police Headquarters and waited. It was a little after nine and the place seemed strangely deserted, shadows crowding in from the corners, falling across the long, narrow desks, filling her with a vague, irrational unease.

Through the frosted glass door of the room on her left, she was aware of movement and the low murmur of voices. After a while, the door opened and a heavily built, greying man in his early forties beckoned to her.

'Superintendent Grant will see you now, Miss Fleming.'

She got to her feet and went in quickly. The room was half in shadow, the only light a green shaded lamp on the desk. It was simply furnished with several filing cabinets and a map of the city on the wall, divisional boundaries marked in red.

Grant was past feeling tired in any conscious sense, but a persistent ache behind one eye and a slight involuntary shiver, which he found quite impossible to control, seemed to indicate that he was under attack from the Asian flu that had already placed something like a fifth of the entire force on the sick list.

He opened a drawer, took three aspirin tablets from a bottle and washed them down with a glass of water. As he reached for a cigarette, he glanced across at the girl on the other side of the desk.

Twenty-seven or -eight and Irish-looking, dark hair razor-cut to the skull in a way he didn't really approve, but it certainly gave her something. The heavy sheepskin coat had cost anything up to forty pounds and the knee-length boots were real leather.

She sat down in the chair Brady brought forward

and crossed her legs, giving Grant the first lift he'd had that night. She arranged her skirt carefully and smiled.

'You don't remember me, Mr Grant?'

'Should I?'

He frowned. Fleming – Jean Fleming. He shook his head and his ugly face split into a smile of quite devastating charm that was one of his most useful assets. 'I must be getting old.'

'I'm Bella Garvald's sister.'

As if she had said some magic word, it all dropped neatly into place. Ben Garvald and the Steel Amalgamated hoist. Eight no, nine years ago. His first big case as a Chief Inspector. His mind jumped back to the house in Khyber Street, to Bella Garvald and her young sister.

'You've changed,' he said. 'As I remember, you were still at the Grammar School waiting to go to college. What was it you wanted to be – a school-teacher?'

'I am,' she said.

'Here in the city?'

She nodded. 'Oakdene Preparatory.'

'Miss Van Heflin's old school? That was on my first beat when I was a young copper. Is she still active? She must be at least seventy.'

'She retired two years ago,' Jean Fleming said. 'It's mine now.'

She was unable to keep a slight edge of pride

11

from her voice and her northern accent became more pronounced.

'A long way from Khyber Street,' Grant said. 'And how's Bella?'

'She divorced Ben not long after he went to prison. Married again last year.'

'I remember now. Harry Faulkner. She did all right for herself there.'

'That's right,' Jean Fleming said calmly. 'And I don't want anything to spoil it for her.'

'Such as?'

'Ben,' she said. 'He was released yesterday.'

'You're sure?'

'With all his remission it would have been last year, but he lost time for breaking from a working party at Dartmoor some years ago.'

Grant blew smoke up to the ceiling. 'You think he'll make trouble?'

'He was difficult about the divorce. That's why he tried to break out when he did. Told Bella he'd never let her go to anyone else.'

'Did she ever visit him again?'

Jean Fleming shook her head. 'There wasn't any point. I went to see him last year when she and Harry got together. I told Ben that she was remarrying, that there was no point in ever trying to contact her again.'

'What was his reaction?'

'He was furious. Wanted to know who it was,

but I refused to tell him. He swore he'd run her down when he got out.'

'Does Faulkner know about all this?'

She nodded. 'Yes, but he doesn't seem particularly bothered. He thinks Ben will never dare show his face here again.'

'He's probably right.'

She shook her head. 'Bella got a letter a few days ago. More a note, really. It just said, *See you soon – Ben.*'

'Has she shown it to her husband?'

Jean Fleming shook her head. 'I know this sounds silly, but it's his birthday and they're throwing a party tonight. An all-night affair. Dancing, cabaret, the lot. I'm looking in myself when I leave here. Bella's put a lot into it. She wouldn't like Ben to spoil things.'

'I see,' Grant said. 'So what do you want us to do? He's served his time. As long as he keeps his nose clean he's a free agent.'

'You could have a word with him,' she said. 'Tell him to stay away. Surely that isn't asking too much?'

Grant swung round in his chair, got to his feet and crossed to the window. He looked down at the lights of the city in the rain below.

'Look at it,' he said, turning to Jean Fleming. 'Seventy square miles of streets, half a million people and eight hundred and twenty-one coppers and that includes the ones who sit behind a desk. By any reasonable standard we need another two hundred and fifty right now.'

'Why can't you get them?'

'You'd be surprised how few men want to spend the rest of their lives working a three-shift system that only gives them one weekend in seven at home with their families. And then the money isn't exactly marvellous, not when you consider what you have to do to earn it. If you don't believe me, try standing outside the Exchange around eleven o'clock on a Saturday night when the pubs are turning out. A good copper earns his week's money in an hour down there.'

'Which is a roundabout way of telling me that you can't help.'

'I've got fifty-two detectives under me. At the present time eighteen have got flu and the rest are working an eighty-hour week. You may have noticed how quiet things are around here. That's because Detective Constable Brady and I are the only people in the office at the moment. At the best of times we only run a token squad during the ten till six shift. Tonight, you could say things are thinner than usual.'

'But there must be someone available.'

He laughed harshly and returned to his desk. 'There usually is.'

She got to her feet. 'It'll be all right, then? You'll see to it?'

'We'll check around,' Grant said. 'It shouldn't be too difficult to find him if he's in town. I can't promise much, but we'll do what we can.'

She fumbled in her bag and took out a card. 'I'll be at Bella's place in St Martin's Wood for an hour or two. After that, I'll be at home. I'm living in Miss Van Heflin's old flat at the school. The number's there.'

She turned to the door. As Brady moved to open it for her, Grant said, 'One thing I don't understand. Why you? Why not Bella?'

Jean Fleming turned slowly. 'You don't remember her very well, do you? She was never much of a one for positive action about anything. If it was left to her she'd just pretend Ben Garvald didn't exist and hope for the best. But this time, that's not good enough, because if anything, I stand to lose even more than she does. A scandal could ruin me, Mr Grant, destroy everything I've worked for. We've come a long way from Khyber Street, you said that yourself. Too far to be dragged back now.'

When she turned and went through the main office, she found that she was trembling. She didn't bother with the lift, but hurried down the three flights of marble stairs to the ground floor and out through the revolving door into the portico at the front of the Town Hall.

She leaned against one of the great stone pillars that towered into the night above her and a gust of wind kicked rain into her face in an oddly menacing manner, ice-cold, like the fear that rose inside her.

'Damn you, Ben Garvald! Damn you to hell!' she said fiercely and plunged down the steps.

'Quite a girl,' Brady said.

Grant nodded. 'And then some. She couldn't be anything else to survive a place like Khyber Street.'

'Do you think there's anything in it, sir?'

'Could be. They didn't come much tougher than Ben Garvald in his day. I don't think nine years of Parkhurst and the Moor will have improved him any.'

'I never knew him personally,' Brady said. 'I was pounding a beat in "C" Division in those days. Had he many friends?'

'Not really. He was always something of a lone wolf. Most people were afraid of him if anything.'

'A real tearaway?'

Grant shook his head. 'That was never Garvald's style. Controlled force – violence when necessary, that was his motto. He was a commando in Korea. Invalided out in '51 with a leg wound. Left him with a slight limp.'

'Sounds a real hard case. Shall I get his papers?'

'First we need someone to handle him.' Grant pulled a file forward, opened it quickly and ran his fingers down a list. 'Graham's still on that rape case at Moorend. Varley went to a factory break-in Maske Lane way an hour ago. Gregory, sick. Lawrence, sick. Forbes, gone to Manchester as a witness in that fraud case coming up tomorrow.'

'What about Garner?'

'Still helping out in "C" Division. They haven't got a plain clothes man capable of standing on his own two feet out there at the moment.'

'And every man a backlog of thirty or more cases at least to work through,' Brady said.

Grant got to his feet, walked to the window and stared down into the rain. 'I wonder what the bloody civilians would say if they knew that tonight we've only got five out in the whole of Central Division.'

Brady coughed. 'There's always Miller, sir.'

'Miller?' Grant said blankly.

'Detective Sergeant Miller, sir,' Brady stressed the title slightly. 'I heard he finished the course at Bramshill last week.'

There was nothing obvious in his tone and yet Grant knew what was implied. Under the new regulations any constable who successfully completed the one year Special Course at the Police College at Bramshill House had to be promoted substantive sergeant immediately on returning to his force, a source of much bitterness to long-serving police officers who had either come up the hard way or were still awaiting promotion.

'I was forgetting him. He's the bloke with the

law degree, isn't he?' Grant said, not because he needed the information, but mainly to see what the other man's reaction would be.

'So they tell me,' Brady replied, a knife edge to his voice that carried with it all the long-serving officer's contempt for the 'book man.'

'I've only met him once. That was when I was on the interviewing panel that considered his application for Bramshill. His record seemed pretty good. Three years on the pavement in Central Division so he must have seen life. As I remember, he was first on the spot after the Leadenhall Street bank raid. It was after that the old man decided to transfer him to the CID. He did a year in "E" Division with Charlie Parker. Charlie thinks he's got just about everything a good copper needs these days.'

'Including a brother with enough money to see him all right for fancy cars,' Brady said. 'He turned up for parade once in an E-type Jag. Did you know about that?'

Grant nodded. 'I also heard he took Big Billy McGuire into the gym and gave him the hiding of his life after Billy had let the air out of the tyres on the same car. They tell me that Billy says he can use himself and that's praise from a master.'

'Fancy tricks, big words,' Brady said contemptuously. 'Can he catch thieves, that's the point.'

'Charlie Parker seems to think so. He wanted him back in "E" Division.'

Brady frowned quickly. 'Where's he going, then?'

'He's joining us,' Grant said. 'The old man gave me the word this afternoon.'

Brady took a deep breath and swallowed back his anger. 'Roses all the way for some people. It took me nineteen years, and at that I'm still a constable.'

'That's life, Jack,' Grant said calmly. 'Miller's supposed to be on leave till Monday.'

'Can I roust him out?'

'I don't see why not. If he's coming to work for us, he might as well get started. His phone number's on the file. Tell him to report in straight away. No excuses.'

A slight, acid smile burned the edges of Brady's mouth and he turned away with his small triumph. As the door closed, Grant lit another cigarette and walked to the window.

A good man, Jack Brady. Solid, dependable. Give him an order and he'd follow it to the letter which was why he was still a Detective Constable, would be till the day he retired.

But Miller was something different. Miller and his kind were what they needed – needed desperately if they were ever to cope with a situation that got more out of hand month by month.

He went back to his chair, stubbed out his cigarette and started to work his way through the mountain of paper work that littered his desk.

3

The houses in Fairview Avenue were typical of the wealthy town dweller. Large without being mansions, each standing remotely in a sea of green lawn. The knowledge that Nick Miller lived in one of these did nothing to improve Jack Brady's temper.

Four Winds was at the end, a late-Victorian town house in grey stone with a half-moon drive and double entrance. Brady drove in, parked his old Ford at the door, got out and rang the bell.

After a while, the door was opened by a slim, greying man of about his own age. He had sharp, decisive features and wore heavy rimmed library spectacles that gave him a deceptively scholarly air.

'Yes, what is it?' He sounded impatient and Brady noticed that he was holding a hand of cards against his right thigh.

'I'm from the Police Department. I've been trying

to get hold of Detective Sergeant Miller, but I can't seem to get any reply. Is your phone out of order?'

The other man shook his head. 'Nick has his own flat over the garage block at the back and a separate phone goes with it. As far as I know, he should be in. I'm his brother – Phil Miller. You want him for something?'

'You could say that.'

'I thought he was on leave till next Monday?'

'So did he. Can I go round?'

'Help yourself. You can't miss it. The fire escape by the main garage door will take you straight up.'

Brady left him there, went back down the steps and followed the gravel drive round the side of the house to a rear courtyard illuminated by a period gas lamp bracketed to the wall above the back door.

The sliding doors of the garage were partially open and he went in and switched on the light. There were three cars parked side by side. A Zodiac, the famous E-type Jaguar and a green Mini-Cooper.

The anger which suddenly boiled inside him was something he found impossible to control. He switched off the light quickly, went out and climbed the iron fire escape to the landing above.

Nick Miller came awake to the sharp, insistent buzzing of the door bell. For a little while he lay there staring up at the ceiling, trying to collect his thoughts, then he threw back the blankets and swung his legs to the floor. He got to his feet, padded into the living-room, switching on a table lamp as he passed, and opened the front door.

Brady took in the black silk pyjamas with the Russian neck and gold buttons, the monogram on the pocket and then his eyes moved up to the face. It was handsome, even aristocratic with sharply pointed chin, high cheekbones and eyes so dark that all light died in them.

At any other time, those eyes would have given him pause, but the frustration and anger boiling inside had taken the sharp edge from his judgement.

'You're Miller?' he said incredulously.

'That's right.'

'Detective Constable Brady. You certainly took your own sweet time answering.' Brady brushed past him. 'Is it the butler's night off or something?'

Nick shut the door and moved towards the fire-place. He opened a silver box that stood on a side table, selected a cigarette and lit it from a Queen Anne table-lighter.

'If you could get to the point,' he said patiently. 'I'd been hoping for an early night.'

'You've had that for a start. Superintendent Grant wants you down at Headquarters. Seems he has a use for your valuable services.' Brady walked across to the telephone which was off the hook and replaced it. 'No wonder I couldn't get a bloody answer.' He swung round angrily. 'I've been trying to ring you for the past half hour.'

'You're breaking my heart.' Miller ran a hand over his chin. 'Anyway, no sense in you hanging around. I'll see you down there. I'll use my own car.'

'Which one, the Rolls?' As Nick moved past him, Brady grabbed his arm. 'The old man said on the double.'

'Then he'll have to wait,' Nick said calmly. 'I'm going to have a shower then a shave, because I need them. You can tell him I'll be there in half an hour.'

With surprising ease he pulled himself free and turned away again and all Brady's anger and frustration flooded out of him in a torrent of rage. He pulled Nick round and gave him a violent shove.

'Just who in the hell do you think you are? You jump up out of nowhere after only five years in the force with your bloody degree and your fancy cars, write your way through an examination and they make you a sergeant. Christ, in that rig-out you look more like a third-rate whoremaster.'

He looked around the luxuriously furnished room, at the thick carpets, the coloured sheepskin rugs and expensive furniture and thought of his own small semi-detached house. A police dwelling on one of the less desirable slum clearance estates on the other side of the river where men like himself and their families lived in a state of perpetual siege.

The irrational anger which he was by now quite unable to control, bubbled out of him. 'And look at this place. More like the waiting room of one of those Gascoigne Square knocking shops.'

'You would know, presumably?' Nick said.

His face had gone very white, had changed completely. The skin was clear and bloodless, the crisp hair in a point to the forehead, the eyes staring through Brady like glass.

They should have warned him, but Brady was long since past the point where reason had any say in the matter. He reached out, grabbing at the black tunic, the silk ripping in his hands and then pain coursed through him like liquid fire and he staggered, a cry rising in his throat as he swung on his right arm, quite helpless.

The pressure was released and he sagged to one knee, and almost at once the pain left him. He got to his feet, dazed, rubbing his right arm in an attempt to restore some feeling to numbed muscle and nerve and looked into the dark, devil's face. Nick smiled gently.

'You need brains for everything, even the heavy

stuff, these days. You made a mistake, Dad. You weren't the first and you won't be the last, but don't speak to me like that again. Next time I'll throw you down the fire escape. Now get out – and that's an order, *Detective Constable Brady*!'

Brady turned, wordless, and stumbled to the door. It closed behind him and Nick stood there listening to the sound of the feet descending the iron fire escape. He sighed heavily, and went into the bathroom.

He stripped the torn tunic from his body and stood looking into the mirror for a while, waiting for the coolness to thaw inside him. After a moment or two he laughed shakily, opened the glass fronted door of the shower cubicle and turned it on.

When he stepped out five minutes later and reached for a towel, he found his brother leaning in the door holding the torn tunic.

'What happened?'

'A difference of opinion, that's all. Brady's the sort who's been around for a long time. He finds it difficult to get used to someone like me jumping the queue.'

Phil Miller tossed the tunic into a corner and swore softly. 'Why go on, Nick? I could use you in the business right now. We're developing all the time, you know that. Why waste yourself?'

Nick moved past him into the bedroom, opened the sliding door of the wardrobe which occupied one side of the room and took down a dark blue worsted suit and freshly laundered white linen shirt. He laid them across the bed and started to dress.

'I happen to like what I'm doing, Phil, and all the Bradys in the Force won't make me change my mind. I'm in and I'm in to stay. The sooner they accept that, the better it will be for all of us.'

Phil shrugged and sat on the edge of the bed, watching him. 'I wonder what the old lady would say if she was still alive. All her plans, all her hopes and you end up a copper.'

Nick grinned at him in the mirror as he quickly knotted a dark blue knitted tie in heavy silk. 'She'd enjoy the joke, Phil. Probably is doing right now.'

'I thought you were supposed to be on leave till Monday?'

Nick shrugged. 'Something must have come up. I was talking to Charlie Parker from "E" Division this afternoon. He was telling me recruiting's hit an all-time low. We're better than two hundred men under establishment. On top of that, God knows how many are on their backs with this Asian flu that's going around.'

'So they need Nick Miller. But why now? What kind of a time is this for a man to be going to work?'

Nick took a dark blue Swedish raincoat from the wardrobe. 'We do it all the time, Phil. You should know that by now. Ten p.m. till six in the morning. The Graveyard Shift.' He grinned as he belted the coat around his waist. 'What would you do if someone turned over one of the shops right now?'

His brother raised a hand defensively and got to his feet. 'All right, you've made your point. So the great Nick Miller goes out into the night to defend society. Watch yourself, that's all I ask. Anything can happen these days.'

'And usually does.' Nick grinned. 'Don't worry, Phil, I can look after myself.'

'See you do. I don't want any phone calls around four in the morning asking me to come down to the Infirmary. Ruth and the kids would take it pretty hard. For some strange reason they seem to think a lot of you.'

'All we need now are violins.' Nick adjusted the peak of the dark blue semi-military rain cap over one eye and turned. 'Will I do?'

'You'll do all right,' Phil said. 'I'm not sure what for, but you'll do.'

Nick grinned and punched him in the shoulder. 'With any kind of luck I might manage breakfast with you.'

He moved to the door and as he opened it, Phil called sharply, 'Nick!'

'What is it?'

Phil sighed heavily and something seemed to go

out of him. 'Nothing. Nothing at all. Just watch it, that's all.'

'I always do.'

He turned and went out into the night, clattering down the fire escape to the cobbled yard, a strange restless excitement surging up inside him at the prospect of being back on the job after a year of space.

Phil stood in the centre of the living room, a slight frown on his face, and beneath him from the garage came a sudden surge of power as an engine roared into life. As he opened the door, the little Mini-Cooper moved across the yard into the drive and disappeared round the corner of the house.

He stood there in the rain at the top of the iron stairway listening to the sound of it fade into the distance on the run down the hill towards the city. And when the silence came, he was afraid. For the first time since he was a little boy he was really and truly afraid.

4

The wind howled fiercely around the corner of the Town Hall and hail rattled the windows of the Information Room.

'God help any poor lad walking the pavement on a night like this,' Grant said as the Duty Inspector turned from the telephone.

'It keeps the other lot indoors as well, sir,' the inspector pointed out. 'One good thing about this flu. It's no respecter of persons. There are just as many villains on their backs tonight as our lads. I can tell that by the 999 calls. Only five so far. We're usually good for thirty at least by this time.'

'A good thing, too, with only four mobiles out to cover the city.' Grant looked down at the great map in the well below with the green and red lights flashing. It was just after ten and he sighed. 'Anyway, don't start counting your chickens. The boozers aren't out yet. We might see some fun then.'

He went into the corridor and met Brady on his way up from the basement where the teleprinter was housed. 'Anything from C.R.O.?'

'They confirm he was released yesterday morning. That's all.'

'What about Miller?'

'No sign of him yet.'

They moved into the main CID office and Grant snorted. 'Taking his bloody time, I must say. You'd better get all the relevant stuff out of the file ready for him then, Jack. We've wasted enough time already.'

'I'll be in Records if you want me,' Brady said and moved out.

Grant paused to light a cigarette and went into his office. Nick was standing by the window looking out into the night. He turned quickly and smiled.

'Good evening, sir.'

Grant took in the highly polished Chelsea boots, the hand-stitched raincoat, the white collar and last of all, the continental raincap.

He took a deep breath. 'What in the hell is that thing on your head?'

Nick took it off with a slight smile. 'This, sir? It's what the Germans call a *Schildtmütze*. Everyone will be wearing them soon.'

'God save us from that,' Grant said, sitting behind his desk.

'Something wrong, sir?'

'Oh, no, if you want to go around looking like one of those burks who stands behind the good-looking bird in the adverts in the women's magazines, good luck to you.'

'As a matter of fact, that's exactly how I do want to look, sir,' Nick replied calmly.

Grant glanced up sharply, suddenly conscious that he was being taken by this supremely confident young man and discovering at the same moment – and this was the most surprising thing of all – that he didn't really mind.

He started to smile and Nick smiled right back at him.

'All right, damn you, one point each. Now sit down and let's get started.'

Nick unbuttoned his coat, sat in the chair opposite and lit a cigarette as Grant continued. 'Brady's getting you all the files you'll need for background on this one, but these are the main facts. Nine years ago, Ben Garvald, one of our better known citizens, went down the steps for a ten stretch. He was released from Wandsworth yesterday morning.'

'And you're expecting him back?'

'His wife is, his ex-wife I should say. That's Bella Garvald. She divorced Ben and married Harry Faulkner five years ago.'

'Harry Faulkner the bookie?'

'Never let him hear you call him that, son. Turf Accountant sounds better. He hasn't soiled his hands with a ready money bet in years. Got his fingers in all sorts of pies these days. Even runs his own football pool.'

'That isn't all he runs,' Nick said. 'From what I remember when I was on the pavement in Central Division, he owned half the cat houses in Gascoigne Square.'

Grant shook his head quickly. 'Try proving it, and in any case, that isn't what we're interested in tonight. It's Ben Garvald we're after.'

'He's in town?'

'That's what I want you to find out and in a hurry. Apparently he made the usual threats to his wife when the divorce went through. She's afraid he's going to show up and spoil her rich full life. Especially tonight. She's throwing a big party for Harry at their place in St Martin's Wood. It's his birthday.'

'How touching,' Nick said. 'She's made an official complaint?'

'Her sister has. That's a Jean Fleming. She's a teacher. Runs her own prep school in Oakdene on the York Road near the city boundary.'

Nick had pulled Grant's desk pad forward and was making rapid notes and now he looked up sharply, a frown on his face. 'Fleming – Jean and Bella Fleming. I wonder if they could be the same?'

'They were both raised in Khyber Street, that's on the south side of the river.'

'That's it,' Nick said. 'My mother kept a shop on the Hull Road just around the corner from Khyber Street. I lived there till I was ten, then we moved to a bigger place in Brentwood.'

'You remember them?'

'I couldn't forget Bella. She was the best known tart in the district. Half the population did nothing else except wait for her to walk by. One of life's great experiences. I was too young, I didn't know what was happening to me. I do now.'

'And never been the same since,' Grant said. 'What about Jean?'

Nick shrugged. 'Just a scrawny kid about my own age. I don't think we ever did more than pass the time of day. They didn't use our shop. My old lady wouldn't give credit.'

The door opened and Brady came in, a pile of files under his arm. He ignored Nick and said to Grant, 'Where do you want these?'

'In the outer office.' Grant looked enquiringly at Nick. 'Need any help? You haven't got much time.'

'Up to you,' Nick said, ignoring Brady.

'All right, Jack can give you a hand for half an hour. If you want any advice, just come in.'

He pulled a file forward and Nick got to his feet and walked into the outer office. As he took off his raincoat and hung it on a stand, Brady dropped the files on one of the desks.

'What do you want me to do?' he said woodenly.

'That depends,' Nick said. 'What have you got there?'

'Garvald's personal file and the files on everyone else who was close to him.'

'Fine,' Nick said. 'I'll take Garvald myself. You start making abstracts of the others.'

Brady didn't argue. He left Garvald's file on the desk, picked up the rest, and went to his own desk in the corner by the window and started to work immediately.

Nick opened Garvald's file and examined the ID card. The face which stared out at him was tough, even ruthless, but there was strength there and intelligence, even a suggestion of humour in the slight quirk at one side of the mouth.

As usual, the card carried the briefest of details and referred only to the offence and charges for which Garvald had last been sent down, namely factory breaking and the stealing of £15,817, the property of Steel Amalgamated Ltd. of Sheffield.

The story contained in the confidential file attached was even more interesting.

Ben Garvald had served for two years in the Marine Commando during the war, being demobilized in 1946. Three months later he was sentenced to one year's imprisonment for conspiracy to steal.

A charge of conspiracy to rob the mails had been dropped for lack of evidence in 1949, and in 1950 he had been recalled from the reserve to fight in Korea. A bullet in the leg had brought him home in the early part of 1951 with a permanent limp and a 33⅓ per cent disability pension.

Between then and his final conviction in June 1956, he had been questioned by the police on no less then twenty-seven occasions in connection with indictable offences.

The door to Grant's office opened and he came out, a cigarette dangling between his lips. 'Got a light?' Nick struck a match and the Superintendent sat on the edge of the desk. 'How are you getting on?'

'Quite a character,' Nick said. 'From the looks of this, they've tried to hang about every charge in the book on him at one time or another.'

'Except for living on immoral earnings and that sort of thing, you're probably right,' Grant said. 'A funny bloke, Ben Garvald. Every villain in town was frightened to death of him and yet where women were concerned, he was like someone out of one of those books they like reading. He treated Bella like a princess.'

'Which would explain why he was so cut up when she decided to divorce him. I've just got to the entry on his last job, the one he got sent down for.'

'I can save you some time there,' Grant said. 'I handled it myself at this end. Garvald and three associates lifted over fifteen thousand quid from the Steel Amalgamated works in Birmingham. Wages for the following day. The daft beggars never learn and I don't mean Garvald and his pals. Anyway, they didn't hit the nightwatchman hard enough, he raised the alarm and Birmingham police sewed the city up tight.'

'Too late?'

'Not quite. There were two cars. One of them crashed and went up like a torch taking a well-known peterman called Jack Charlton and his driver up with it.'

'And Garvald?'

'He and the other bloke crashed a road block and got clean away. We lifted Garvald next day and the nightwatchman picked him out at an identity parade with no trouble at all.'

'And the money?'

'Garvald said it was in the other car.'

'A likely story.'

'Strangely enough I was inclined to believe him.

We certainly found traces of some of it in the ashes. That's as far as we got anyway and we didn't get the other man.'

'So Garvald kept his mouth shut?'

'True to the code. Went down the steps like a man.'

'The bloke who was with him in the car that night, did you have any fancy ideas at the time?'

'Plenty and they all came down to Fred Manton.'

'Manton?' Nick frowned. 'Doesn't he run that place in Gascoigne Square – The Flamingo Club?'

Grant nodded. 'He and Garvald were partners in a small club on the other side of the river at the time of the robbery. Trouble was, too many customers came forward to swear that Fred Manton had been in the club all night and one or two of them were pretty respectable citizens.'

'Has Manton got any form?'

Brady crossed the office and placed a foolscap sheet in front of him. 'There's an abstract of his file.'

Nick examined it quickly. *Frederick Manton, 44, club owner, Gascoigne Square, Manningham. Four previous convictions including thirty months for conspiracy to steal; larceny; loitering with intent. On eighteen occasions the police had thought he might be able to help them with their enquiries, but Manton had always managed to walk right down the Town Hall steps again.*

'Let's suppose you were right about Manton after all,' he said to Grant. 'And that the cash from the Steel Amalgamated job didn't go up in smoke. A place like the Flamingo must have cost a lot to get started. It would be understandable if Garvald turned up and wanted a slice of the cake.'

'Ingenious, but there's only one fault.' Grant got to his feet and moved towards his office. 'Harry Faulkner owns the Flamingo Club. Fred Manton's just hired help as far as he's concerned and don't try to drag Harry Faulkner into this. His cars are worth fifteen grand alone.'

The door closed behind him and Nick looked up at Brady. 'What about the rest?'

'There are nine here, all people he was pretty thick with,' Brady said. 'Five of them are in one nick or another. Four are still around. They're on top.'

He dropped the abstracts on Nick's desk, walked to Grant's door, opened it and leaned inside. 'All right if I take my break now?'

Grant glanced at his watch. 'Fine, Jack, see you back here about midnight.'

Brady closed the door, took his raincoat from the stand, and pulled it on as he went out into the corridor. He stood at the wire grill of the lift shaft impatiently pressing the button.

If Ben Garvald *was* in town, there was one place he was bound to go, one person he was certain to visit. That much was obvious to anyone with any experience and if he was there, he – Jack Brady – would have him back at Headquarters within an hour at the outside while that clever sod Miller walked the pavements looking for him. It would be interesting to see what Grant had to say then. When he got into the lift, he was trembling with excitement.

5

Round about the time Jean Fleming was having her interview with Grant, Garvald was dropping off a truck at a bus stop on the North Circular Ring Road that linked the city with the A1. Ten minutes later, he boarded the first bus to come along and left it half a mile from the city centre, going the rest of the way on foot.

The journey from London could have taken no more than a comfortable four hours in a Pullman car, but that would have been too conspicuous an entrance into the city under the circumstances.

There were people to see, things to be done, accounts to be settled – notably Sammy Rosco's – but first he needed a base from which to operate.

He found what he was looking for without too much trouble, a third-rate hotel in a back street near the centre of town. When he went in, a woman in a blue nylon overall was sitting behind the reception desk reading a magazine. She could have been anywhere between twenty-five and thirty with dark curling hair and bold black eyes.

Garvald rested an elbow on the desk. 'And who might you be?'

She closed the magazine, a spark of interest in her eyes and responded to his mood. 'A poor Irish girl trying to make an honest living in a hard land.'

'God save the good work,' Garvald said. 'You can give me a room for a start. A room with a bath.'

'All our rooms have a bath,' she said calmly. 'There's one at the end of the corridor on each floor.'

She took a key down from the board, lifted the flap of the reception desk and led the way up the stairs.

The room was no better and no worse than he had expected with the usual heavy Victorian furniture and a worn carpet. A modern washbasin with tiled splashback had been fitted in one corner. He dropped his holdall on a chair, walked to the window and looked down into the street as the woman turned back the bedspread.

'Will that be all?' she said.

Garvald turned. 'Any chance of a drink?'

'We aren't licensed. There's a pub down the street.'

He shook his head. 'Not to worry. I could do with an early night, anyway.'

She dropped the key on the dressing-table.

'Anything you want, just ring. I'm on call all night.'

Garvald grinned. 'The thought of that's more than flesh and blood can stand.'

She smiled right back at him and the door closed behind her. Garvald's grin disappeared and he lit a cigarette, sat on the edge of the bed and leafed through the phone book. There was no entry for Sammy Rosco and he sat there for a while, a slight frown on his face, trying to think of someone he could trust. Someone from the old days who might still be around.

He discarded the names as they came to him one by one, and was left finally with only Chuck Lazer, the quiet American who'd been resident pianist at the old One-Spot when Garvald and Fred Manton had run it together.

But Chuck would never have stayed on, couldn't have. He'd have gone back to the States years before, so much was obvious and yet, when Garvald looked in the phone book again, the name jumped out at him. Chuck Lazer – 15 Baron's Court.

He reached for the telephone, hesitated, then changed his mind. This was something that would be handled better in person. He pulled on his hat and left, locking the door behind him.

At the head of the stairs he hesitated, then moved

along the corridor and tried a door at the end. It opened on to a narrow flight of dark stairs and he went down quickly, a stale smell of cooking rising to meet him through the darkness. At the bottom, he found himself in a dimly lit passage facing a door. He opened it and stepped into the alley at the side of the hotel.

To save time he took a taxi from a rank in City Square. Lazer's address was not far from the University, a district of tall, decaying Victorian houses which had, in the main, been converted into cheap boarding houses or flats.

Garvald followed a narrow path through an overgrown garden and mounted several steps to a large porch. He could hear laughter from somewhere inside and music as he examined the name cards beneath the row of bell pushes.

Chuck Lazer had Flat 5 on the third floor and Garvald opened the door and moved into the hall. As he closed it behind him, a door on his right opened, music and laughter flooding out and a young man with tousled hair and a fringe of beard emerged, carrying a crate of empty bottles.

Garvald paused at the bottom of the stairs. 'Chuck Lazer wouldn't happen to be in there, would he?'

'Good God, no,' the young man said. 'Booze and bints, that's all we go in for, old man. Not Chuck's style at all. You'll probably find him in his pit.'

He disappeared along the corridor and Garvald mounted the stairs quickly, a slight frown on his face, wondering what all that was supposed to mean.

It was strangely remote from things up there on the third floor and the music sounded faint and unreal like something from another world. Garvald checked the card on the door, listened for a moment, then knocked. There was no reply and when he reached for the handle, the door opened to his touch.

The stench was overpowering, a compound of stale sweat, urine and cooking odours mixed with some other indefinable essence that for the moment escaped him.

He switched on the light and looked around the cluttered, filthy room to the narrow bed against the far wall and the half naked man who sprawled on it face down. Garvald opened a window wide, drawing the damp, foggy air deep into his lungs, then lit a cigarette and turned to the bed again.

On top of a small bedside locker were littered the gear which told the story. A hypodermic with several needles, most of them dirty and blunted. Heroin and cocaine bottles, both empty, a cup still half-full of water, a small glass bottle, its base discoloured from the match flame and a litter of burned-out matches.

The bare arm hanging over the side of the bed was dotted with needle marks, some of them scabbed over where infection had set in. Garvald took a deep breath and turned Lazer on his back.

The American's face was fleshless, gaunt from malnutrition, a dark beard giving him the appearance of an emaciated saint. He stirred once and Garvald slapped him across the face. The eyelids fluttered in an uncontrollable muscular spasm, then opened, the dark eyes staring blindly into an eternity of hell.

'Chuck, it's me,' Garvald said. 'Ben Garvald.'

Lazer stared blankly at him and Garvald placed his cigarette between the man's lips. Lazer inhaled deeply and started to cough in great, wrenching spasms that seemed to tear at his entire body. When he finally managed to stop, he was shivering uncontrollably and his nose was running.

Garvald threw a blanket over his shoulders. 'It's me, Chuck, Ben Garvald,' he said again.

'I read you, loud and clear, Dad. Loud and clear.' Lazer started to shiver again and pulled the blanket up around his neck. 'Christ, I need a fix. Oh, sweet Jesus, I need a fix.' He took a great shuddering breath as if making a real effort to get control and looked up at Garvald. 'Long time no see, Ben.'

'Thanks for all the letters.'

'There was never anything worth saying.'

'Oh, I don't know. What about Bella?'

'A harlot, Benny boy. A lovely whore, dancing with tinkling cymbals to the tune of whoever tossed the largest gold piece.'

'They tell me she got married again.'

'The pot of gold, Benny boy. The end of the rainbow. Didn't you know?'

'Who's the lucky man?'

'Harry Faulkner.'

'Harry Faulkner?' Ben frowned. 'He must be pushing sixty.'

'And then some, but he's a big man these days, Ben. A big man. He has a finger in just about anything that pays off and he isn't too particular. He and Bella live in a replica of Haroun al Raschid's palace out at St. Martin's Wood in the gin and tonic belt.'

'Is Fred Manton still around?'

'Sure, he works for Harry these days. Runs a club called the Flamingo in Gascoigne Square. I play the piano for him whenever I remember.' He moaned suddenly and again his body was racked by uncontrollable shivering. 'Christ, but I need that fix.' He struggled for breath, his teeth chattering. 'What time is it?'

'About ten fifteen.'

Lazer's face tightened visibly. 'Too late for evening surgery. That means I can't get a prescription till the morning.'

'You're a registered addict?'

Lazer nodded. 'The only reason I didn't go back to the States years ago. Over there, they'd sling me in the can. Here, at least they allow me to exist, courtesy of the Health Service.'

'How long have you been on this stuff?' Garvald said, picking up the empty heroin bottle.

Lazer bared his teeth in a ghastly grin. 'Too long to be able to get through the night without a fix, Benny boy.'

'You know where you can get one?'

'Sure, outside the all-night chemist's in City Square. Plenty of junkies getting their evening surgery prescriptions filled, but it could take money. Something I'm fresh out of.'

Garvald took a wallet from his breast pocket and counted ten one-pound notes out carefully on top of the bedside locker.

'Enough?'

'Plenty.' Lazer's eyes were suddenly full of light and he reached for the notes.

Garvald covered them with one large hand. 'Sammy Rosco, Chuck. Where would I find him?'

'Sammy?' Lazer looked surprised. 'He works for Manton around the clubs.'

'The Flamingo?'

'With his mug?' Lazer shook his head. 'Fred manages one or two other places for Faulkner, dives mostly. Bad booze and worse women. You know the sort of thing. Sammy goes where they need him most. Barman and chucker-out, that's his style. I think he's at Club Eleven this week.'

'He and Wilma still together?'

'He couldn't manage without her. Mind you, things haven't been the same since the Act pushed 'em all in off the streets. She mostly works from the house now.' He frowned desperately, trying to remember. 'Carver Street. Yes, that's right – Carver Street. I don't know the number, but it's about half way along, next door to a shop with its window boarded up. The whole street's due down soon.'

Garvald gathered the notes in one quick movement and pushed them into Lazer's open hand, closing the fingers tightly. 'Good man, Chuck, I'll see you.'

'At whose funeral?'

Ben Garvald turned in the doorway and smiled briefly. 'I haven't quite made my mind up yet. When I do, I'll let you know. You'd make a good mute.'

The door closed behind him. For a little while Lazer crouched there on the bed, the blanket wrapped tightly around him, the money clutched in his right hand and then, in one quick, positive movement that started off a chain action, he jumped up and started to get dressed.

6

Carver Street was a row of crumbling terrace houses near the river in a slum area which, as Chuck Lazer had said, was due for demolition.

Garvald found the shop with the boarded window about half-way along. The house next to it looked as if it might fall down at any moment and he followed a narrow tunnelled passage that brought him into a backyard littered with empty tins and refuse of every description.

He stumbled up four steps and knocked at the door. After a while, footsteps approached, it opened a few inches and a woman's voice said, 'Who is it?'

'I'm looking for Sam,' Garvald said. 'Sammy Rosco. I'm an old friend of his.'

'He isn't in.'

The slight German accent that had been one of her great attractions when he first knew her was still marked, and he moved closer to the door.

'It's Ben, Wilma. Ben Garvald.'

There was a sudden, sharp intake of breath, a slight pause and then the chain rattled and the door opened. As he stepped into the dark corridor, a hand reached for his face and arms pulled him close.

'Ben, *liebling*. I can't believe it. Is it really you?'

She drew him along the dark corridor and into a room at the far end. It was reasonably clean and comfortable with a carpet on the floor and a double bed against the far wall.

She turned to face him, a large heavily built woman running dangerously to seed, make-up too heavy, the flesh under the chin sagging. Only the incredible straw coloured hair was as he remembered it and he smiled.

She coloured and her head went back. 'So, I look older. It's been a long time.'

'You've still got the most beautiful hair I've ever seen.'

Something glowed deep in her eyes, and for a moment she was once again the young, slender German girl that Sammy Rosco had brought home after the war. She moved close to Garvald, her arms sliding up around his neck, and kissed him firmly on the mouth.

'Always, you were worth all of them put together.'

Garvald held her close for a moment, savouring

54

with a conscious pleasure the feel of a woman's body against his own, the first in a long time, then he pushed her firmly away.

'Business, Wilma, business. Is there a drink in the house?'

'The day there isn't will be the day.'

She moved to a cupboard, took out a bottle of gin and two glasses and Garvald sat in a chair at the table. He looked around the room. 'Still on the game?'

She shrugged as she sat in the opposite chair. 'What else can I do?'

'Ever thought of going home?'

'To Bavaria?' She got to her feet, went to a corner by the window, lifted the carpet and produced a white envelope. She opened it and took out a passport which she threw on the table. 'I keep it well out of Sammy's sight. Last time I tried to use it, he beat me up so bad, I was in hospital for a week.'

'You didn't prefer charges?'

'Do me a favour.' She shrugged. 'Since then, I haven't been able to scrape more than a fiver together at any one time. He sees to that. Waits in the kitchen for the clients to go, then he's straight in for the cash.'

Garvald picked up the passport and opened it. 'It's still valid, I see?'

'So what? It's about as much good as a ticket

to the moon.' She swallowed her gin and refilled the glass. 'What brought you back, Ben? There's nothing for you here. I suppose you know Bella married again.'

'So I'm told. Where's Sammy now?'

'The Grosvenor Taps, that's a boozer at the end of the street.'

'Expecting him back?'

She glanced at the clock and nodded. 'They've been closed about five minutes. He usually looks in before going on to work.'

'And where would that be?'

She shrugged. 'Various places. This week he's at Club Eleven, that's a clip joint about half a mile from here that Fred Manton runs for Faulkner.'

'Who's in charge?'

'Molly Ryan.'

'Girls, too, eh?'

Wilma shrugged. 'You know what these places are like. Anything goes. Do you want Sammy for something special?'

Garvald lit another cigarette and blew smoke up at the shaded lamp. 'When I came out of Wandsworth yesterday morning, a couple of hard cases tried to take me, Wilma. They made a bad mistake.' He grinned coldly. 'So did Sammy.'

The outside door crashed open and steps sounded along the corridor. A moment later, Sammy Rosco lurched into the room. He was a squat ox of a man with arms that hung down to his knees. His face was sullen and bloated with whisky and he stood there, swaying, a nasty gleam in his eye.

'What's going on here, then?'

'Someone to see you, Sammy dear,' Wilma said, a deep, ripe pleasure in her voice. 'An old friend.'

Garvald turned his head and smiled gently. 'Now then, Sammy, you old bastard.'

His face was very calm, but the grey eyes, changing constantly like windswept smoke on an autumn day, told Rosco everything he needed to know. He swung round, lurching for the door, but Garvald was even quicker. His hand fastened on Rosco's collar and with a tremendous heave, he sent him crashing across the room.

Rosco came up from the floor in a rush, and Garvald coolly measured the distance and booted him in the stomach. Rosco keeled over with a sigh, falling across the bed, writhing in agony.

Wilma sat watching, no pity in her eyes, and Garvald emptied the gin bottle into his glass, sat down and waited. After a while, Rosco turned, his face the colour of paper.

'Feeling better, Sammy?'

'You get stuffed, you bastard,' Rosco managed to squeeze out.

'That's better,' Garvald said. 'That's a lot better. Now why did you sic those two tearaways on to me yesterday morning?'

'I don't know what in the hell you're talking about.'

In one quick movement, Garvald seized the empty gin bottle by the neck and smashed it across the edge of the table. He leaned forward and held the jagged, vicious weapon under Rosco's chin.

'Maybe you've forgotten, Sammy, but I never liked playing games.'

Sweat sprang to Rosco's brow in great heavy drops and his eyes widened visibly. 'It was Fred, Ben. Fred Manton. He told me to line it up for him. Said he didn't want you back.'

Garvald frowned and all light died in his eyes. 'Why, Sammy? Why would Manton do a thing like that? It doesn't make sense.'

He pushed the bottle forward viciously and Sammy screamed. 'That's all I know. I swear it, Ben.'

Garvald tossed the bottle into the fireplace with a quick gesture, then hauled Rosco to his feet. He opened the man's coat, pulled the wallet from the inside pocket and opened it quickly. There was fifty pounds in five-pound notes, all new. He counted them quickly, then gave Rosco a contemptuous shove towards the door.

'Start running and don't come back.'

Rosco turned in the doorway, opening his mouth to say something, then obviously thought better of it. He stumbled along the corridor in the darkness and, a moment later, the back door banged behind him.

Garvald tossed the fifty pounds on to the table. 'More than enough to get you back home there, Wilma. Unless things have changed since I was around, there are still night expresses to London.'

She flung herself into his arms, straining against him and when she looked up, tears shone brightly in her eyes, smudging the mascara.

'I'll never forget you, Ben Garvald. Never.'

He kissed her once, gave her a quick squeeze and was gone. She stood there listening to him pass through the tunnel at the side of the house, his footsteps fading along the hollow pavement.

She gazed around the room, filled with a sudden hatred of this place, of Sammy Rosco and the wasted years and what they had done to her. Very quickly, she started to pack.

It was almost midnight when she was ready. She pulled on her raincoat, picked up the suitcase, looked round the room briefly for the last time and walked out along the dark passage.

As she reached the door, someone knocked.

Oh, God, no. Oh, dear God, no. The cry rose in her throat and she turned and stumbled back along the dark passage to the room and behind her, the door opened.

She fell on her knees at the fireplace, her fingers scrabbling desperately in the broken glass. They fastened upon a large piece, curved like a dagger and as sharp. She arched her throat striking upwards and was aware of pain, pain like fire that flowed through the arm so that she dropped the glass with a scream. A hand pulled her to her feet, swung her round and sent her staggering across the room to fall across the bed.

She raised an arm to protect her face from the blow that always followed and then lowered it with a tiny whimper because it wasn't Sammy Rosco who stood by the table looking down at her. This was a much younger man, someone she'd never seen before in an expensive blue raincoat with strange, dark eyes that seemed to look right through her.

7

Charles Edward Lazer, 45, musician, 15 Baron's Court. American citizen. Joined RAF October 1939, demobilized June 1946. Rank, F/Lieutenant Navigator. Record – Excellent. Awarded DFC in May 1944. Four previous convictions including conspiracy to steal, suspected person, larceny and illegal possession of drugs. Not deported because of excellent war record and fact of all offences being concerned with subject's addiction to drugs.

Nick went through the facts again in his mind as he waited outside the door in the dimly lit passage. There was no reply to his knock, and when he tried the handle the door opened to his touch.

The window was open, the curtains lifting in the wind, and rain drifted through in a fine spray. Nick looked briefly around the dirty, untidy room, his nostrils flaring at the stench of the unwashed bedding, then he turned, left the room and went downstairs.

The noise from the flat on the ground floor was tremendous, a steady, pulsating beat vibrating through the night as a blues and rhythm group really started to move. Nick knocked on the door a couple of times without getting a reply, opened it and looked inside.

There must have been at least thirty or forty people packed into the room, mainly students from the look of them, eating, drinking, dancing to the three-man group in the corner. In one case even making love on the floor behind the old-fashioned sofa.

A young man with tangled hair and a fringe beard was moving through the crowd, refilling glasses from a large enamel jug. As he turned from one group, he caught sight of Nick and came across.

'Sorry, old man, no gate-crashers. Strictly private this time.'

Nick produced his warrant card and the other's face dropped. 'Now what, for Christ's sake?'

He opened the door and Nick followed him out into the corridor, closing the door behind him, effectively cutting off most of the din.

'No trouble,' he said. 'I'm just trying to trace a bloke who lives upstairs – Chuck Lazer. He wouldn't be inside by any chance?'

The young man grinned, took a cigarette from behind his ear and stuck it in the corner of his mouth. 'Chuck? I should say not! Moves in his own narrow circle, God help him.'

'Is he still on junk?' Nick said.

'As far as I know, but he's a registered user now.' The young man frowned suddenly. 'Look, what *is* all this?'

'Nothing to get worked up about, I'm not trying to hang anything on him. I want his help with a routine enquiry, that's all.'

'That's what you lot always say.'

Nick shrugged. 'Suit yourself.'

He turned towards the door and the young man said quickly: 'Oh, what the hell. He overslept, missed the evening surgery. Someone came looking for him about half an hour ago.'

'What kind of someone?'

'Big man, dirty raincoat, Irish looking.' The young man grinned suddenly. 'That cap's the coolest thing I've seen in years. Where can I get one?'

'Any good men's shop in Hamburg. Did they leave together?'

The young man shook his head. 'Lazer went out about ten minutes ago. I was having five minutes with one of the birds up at the end of the passage when he came down.'

'Was he in a hurry?'

'They always are when they need a fix. I'd say he was on his way round to see his quack about a prescription.'

'And who would that be?'

'Dr Das, just round the corner in Baron's Square. He's about the only one in town who'll take junkies on his list. Say, are you really a copper?'

'As ever was.'

'Crazy!' the young man said, frank admiration in his eyes. 'If I join will they guarantee me a uniform like that?'

'I'll mention it to the Chief Constable in the morning. We'll be in touch.'

'You do that, man.'

He opened the door and returned to his party as Nick went down the steps into the rain. There was a touch of fog in the air, heavy and acrid, catching at the back of the throat, and he climbed behind the wheel of the Mini-Cooper and drove around the corner to Baron's Square.

Dr Das lived at number twenty and a brass plate on the door disclosed the surprising fact, considering the district and circumstances, that he was not only an MD but also a Fellow of the Royal College of Physicians.

Nick rang the bell and after a while heard footsteps approaching. The door was opened by a tall, cadaverous Indian with high cheekbones and serene brown eyes.

'Dr Das?'

'That is correct. What can I do for you?'

'Detective Sergeant Miller, CID. I'm trying to trace a patient of yours, a Mr Lazer. I've just missed him at his home and one of his neighbours thought he might have intended calling on you.'

'Come in, please, Sergeant.'

Nick followed him along the passage and the Indian opened a door at the far end and led the way in. A cheerful fire burned in a polished grate, there was a desk in one corner and the walls were lined with books.

Dr Das took a cheroot from a sandalwood box on the mantelpiece, lit it with a splinter from the fire and turned with a smile. 'You will excuse me not offering you one of these, Sergeant, but the supply is limited and I can only obtain them with great difficulty. You'll find cigarettes on the desk behind you.'

Nick helped himself and the Indian stood with his back to the fire, his face perfectly calm. 'Mr Lazer is in trouble?'

Nick shook his head. 'No question of that at all. It's just that I'm trying to trace someone rather urgently and I think Lazer might be able to help me. I understand he's a drug addict and registered with you.'

'That is perfectly correct,' Das said. 'Mr Lazer has been a patient of mine for two years or more now. I take a particular interest in people in his unfortunate condition. Very few doctors do, I might add.'

'How advanced is Lazer?'

Das shrugged. 'His daily intake is of the order of seven grains of heroin and six grains of cocaine a day. When you appreciate that the normal dose to relieve pain is one-twelfth of a grain of heroin, this indicates the extent of the problem.'

'Can't anything be done?'

'For most patients, I'm afraid not. I have patients who've been "dried-out," as they call it, as many as sixteen or seventeen times. They regress with astonishing ease. The trouble is that most of them have quite crippling personality defects which explains their initial need for drugs, of course.'

'I find that hard to accept where Lazer's concerned,' Nick said. 'I've seen his record. He did rather well with the RAF during the war.'

'Charles Lazer is a particularly tragic case. He first took heroin and cocaine at a party something like three years ago. Apparently he was quite drunk at the time and didn't know what he was doing.'

'And after that he was hooked?'

'I'm afraid so. He's dried-out on two occasions, once for almost five months before regression set in and believe me, that's really quite remarkable.'

'So there's still hope for him?'

Dr Das smiled slightly. 'You seem to have a personal interest here.'

Nick shrugged. 'I've seen his record, I like the sound of him – it's as simple as that. He fought a good war, Dr Das. I'm still old-fashioned enough to think that should count for something. Isn't there anything you can do for him – anything concrete?'

The Indian nodded. 'There is a new method which a colleague of mine in London has enjoyed remarkable success with during the past year. It involves the use of apomorphine and the actual withdrawal of drugs from the patient over a period of some months.'

'And it really works?'

'With co-operation from the patient. Apomorphine is morphine minus a molecule of water. Injected into the patient, it cuts his craving for the drug and prevents the withdrawal symptoms usually associated with any attempt to cut down the daily intake. These can be extremely unpleasant.'

'Have you mentioned this to Lazer yet?'

'I was going to tonight, but he didn't turn up for evening surgery.'

'Isn't it possible that he would come outside surgery hours if his need was urgent enough?'

Das shook his head. 'He'd be wasting his time. My first rule is that I never give prescriptions for drugs outside surgery hours. This may seem harsh to you, but I assure you that firmness and an insistence on some sort of discipline are absolutely essential in handling this type of patient.'

'So Lazer would have to wait till morning surgery and get through the night the best way he could?'

'Highly unlikely.' Das shook his head. 'Unless I'm very much mistaken, he'll make straight for the all-night chemist's in City Square. There are certain to be one or two addicts having their prescriptions for the following day filled and they all know each other in a town of this size. Lazer will borrow or buy a few pills to tide him over till morning.'

'You think I'll find him there?'

'I'm certain of it.'

'I'd better be moving then. I don't want to miss him.'

'I should warn you of one thing,' the Indian said as they moved back along the corridor to the front door. 'After Lazer's first injection, you will notice something of a change in him. Sometimes the subject becomes paranoic with a particular fear where the police are concerned. More often than not, his tongue will simply run away from him or he'll have temporary aural or visual hallucinations. All quite harmless, but disturbing if you aren't used to this sort of thing.'

'I'll bear that in mind.' Nick held out his hand.

'Any time I can help, Sergeant.' The Indian's grip was surprisingly strong. 'Don't hesitate to call.'

The door closed behind him and Nick went down the steps, got into the car quickly and drove away through the heavy rain.

8

Chuck Lazer held on grimly as the beetles started to crawl across his flesh with infinite slowness, setting up a muscular reaction he found impossible to control. He stepped out of the entrance of the all-night chemist's and turned his face to the night sky, the stinging lances of rain giving him some kind of temporary relief.

Behind him, a small wizened man in an old beret and raincoat moved out, unwrapping the package he held in his hands.

Lazer turned quickly. 'Hurry it up, Darko, for Christ's sake. I can't take much more of this.'

The little man opened a pillbox and shook some heroin tablets into Lazer's palm. 'Don't forget where they came from,' he said. 'I'll be in the Red Lizard for coffee around eleven in the morning. You can pay me back then.'

He moved away quickly and Lazer walked to

the kerb. At the same moment, a green Mini-Cooper pulled in beside him. The door swung open and a young man in a spectacular blue raincoat got out.

'Detective Sergeant Miller, Central CID, Lazer. I'd like a word with you. Where can we talk?'

Lazer took in the coat, the strange dark eyes, the military style cap and laughed wildly. 'General, you could be Alexander the Great and Napoleon rolled into one for all I care. Right now, you'll have to take your place in the queue.'

He dodged across the road between two cars, reached the centre island and disappeared down the steps of the public lavatory. Nick judged his moment and went after him.

At the bottom of the steps, the attendant's little office was dark and empty and when he turned the corner into the vast tiled lavatory, he found it deserted except for Lazer who was feverishly wrestling with the handle of one of the stalls at the far end.

As Nick reached him, the American got the door open and lurched inside. He pulled down the seat, ignoring Nick and dropped to one knee, taking several items from his pocket and laying them out.

He took off his raincoat and jacket, pulled back his sleeve and knotted a brown lace around his upper arm in a rough tourniquet to make the veins stand out. He filled a small bottle with water from the pan, dropped in a couple of tablets, struck a match feverishly and held it underneath.

He turned his head, teeth bared in a savage grin, all the agony of existence at this level spilling from his eyes. 'It's a great life if you don't weaken, General.'

He reached for another match, knocked the box to the floor, spilling its contents, and moaned like an animal. Nick took a lighter from his pocket, flicked it into life and held it out without speaking.

Lazer held the flame under the bottle for another couple of minutes and then dropped it quickly and filled his hypodermic.

Four years as a policeman in one of the largest industrial cities in the North of England had hardened Nick Miller to most things, but when that filthy, blunted needle went into Lazer, it went into him also. Blood spurted, Lazer loosened his crude tourniquet and his head went back, eyes closed.

He stayed that way for only a second or two and then his whole body was convulsed. He grabbed at the wall with an exclamation and lurched into Nick who crouched in front of him.

The American stayed that way for a while, head down and then he looked up slowly and managed a ghastly smile. 'The moment of truth, General. Now what was it you wanted?'

9

The club was just around the corner in a side street, the sort of place that had mushroomed by the dozen during the past few years, and Nick remembered it well from his days on the pavement in Central Division.

The big West Indian on the door grinned as they came down the narrow stairs. 'Hi, there, Chuck! How's every little thing? You going to play for us tonight?'

'No can do, Charlie,' Lazer said as he scrawled his name in the book. 'I got a gig someplace later on when I can remember where it is.'

The Negro turned to Nick and immediately something moved in his eyes. Nick held up a hand quickly. 'Strictly pleasure, Charlie. How's business?'

'Fine, Mr Miller. Just fine. Ain't seen you around. I heard you'd left the Force.'

'Just a nasty rumour, Charlie. I'm a sergeant with the Crime Squad now. You'll be seeing a lot of me.'

Charlie grinned, exposing his excellent teeth. 'Not if I can help it, I won't.'

There were no more than half a dozen people in the main bar, all coloured. Lazer raised a hand to the barman and sat down at a mini piano on a dais against the wall. Nick lit a cigarette, pulled forward a chair and sat beside him.

The American's hands crawled across the keys, searching for something in a minor key, finding it after a moment or two, a pulsating, off-beat rhythm that had something of the night and the city mixed in with it.

Nick waited his chance, then moved in with the right hand, blending in expertly. The American turned and grinned his appreciation.

'You've bin there, General. You've bin there.'

They finished with a complex run of chords that had the other people in the bar applauding. The American's eyes glittered excitedly and his face was flushed. When the barman brought two whiskies on a tray with the compliments of the house, he swallowed one down quickly and laughed.

'You've got a soul, General, a golden, shining soul. I can see it drifting around you in a cloud of glory. You're Tatum and Garner rolled into one. If Brubeck heard you, he'd turn his face to the wall and weep tears of pure joy, General. Tears of pure joy.'

'Garvald,' Nick said. 'Ben Garvald.'

Lazer faltered, the spate of words drying momentarily. 'Ben?' he said. 'My old buddy Ben? Sure, I know Ben. He was around my place earlier tonight.' He paused, a worried frown on his face. 'Or was it tonight? Maybe it was some other time.'

'What did he want?' Nick said patiently.

'What did he want? What did old Ben want?' Lazer's mood changed suddenly. He reached for Nick's glass, emptied it, then started to play a Bach prelude with exquisite skill. 'Well, I'll tell you, General. Old Ben wanted to know about his wife, what her new name was and where she lived.'

'And that's all?'

'Then he wanted to know where he could find Sammy.'

'Sammy?'

'Sammy Rosco. He's the strong-arm man at Club Eleven. Lives in Carver Street.'

'Why did Garvald want to see him?'

Lazer changed to a Strauss waltz. 'He didn't mean him any good, General, that's for sure. The Angel of Death walked at his side. The Lord have mercy on the soul of Samuel Rosco, miserable sinner.' He laughed wildly. 'Heh, you know what that creep did, General? Sicked a couple of cheap punks on to Ben in the fog outside Wandsworth. Did *he* make a mistake.'

He was at the high point of his ecstasy, knowing and yet not knowing what he was saying and Nick pushed his advantage.

'What did he want Bella for, Chuck? Was he angry with her?'

'With Bella? Why should he be angry?' The waltz changed into a slow, dragging blues that brought a Negro couple in the corner to their feet to dance. 'He loved that woman, General. He loved her and she threw him overboard and married another man.'

'So maybe he wants to even the score a little.'

'You mean cut her up or something?' The fingers faltered, the melody drifted into silence. 'General, you don't know Ben Garvald. You sure as hell don't know Ben Garvald.' He leaned forward and laid a hand on Nick's shoulder. 'Where women are concerned, he's the softest touch in town.'

'You've made your point.' Nick started to his feet.

Lazer held on tight. 'Why all the interest? You think he's going to have a go at Bella?'

'She does.'

'She's made an official complaint?'

'Something like that.'

'The lousy bitch. After all he did for her. Nine stinking years, then she divorces him and marries an old man with a bag of gold.'

'Life can be hell,' Nick said.

He moved away quickly, aware of Lazer's quick cry, went straight up the stairs without looking back and went along the alley into City Square. Carver Street and Sammy Rosco were obviously next on the agenda and he got behind the wheel of the Mini-Cooper and moved away quickly. Behind him in the entrance to the alley, Lazer paused, a hand raised in a futile gesture as Miller drove off. A match flared in a doorway beside him and Ben Garvald moved out, lighting a cigarette.

'Who's your friend, Chuck?'

Lazer swung round in surprise. Already, the initial jolt of the drug was wearing thin and he was dropping fast towards a level more consistent with normal behaviour.

'Where in the hell did you spring from?'

'I wanted to see you again. Remembered what you said about the all-night chemist's in City Square. You and the character in the blue coat and fancy cap were standing at the kerb when I came round the corner. Who is he?'

'A copper, Ben. Detective Sergeant.' Lazer searched his memory. 'Miller. That's it – Miller.'

'You're joking,' Garvald said. 'I've never seen a peeler that looked like him before. What did he want?'

'You, Ben,' Lazer said. 'He wanted to know if I knew where you were.'

'Did he say why?'

Lazer tried again. 'Bella, that's it, Bella. She doesn't want you around.'

'She's got her nerve,' Garvald said. 'What did you tell this peeler, then?'

And Lazer, his mind chilling as the ecstasy ebbed away, couldn't remember. Garvald saw the situation for what it was and nodded quickly.

'Forget it, Chuck. It doesn't matter. I'm clean as a whistle and those sods up there at the Town Hall know it. In any case, I've more important things to think about. Where would I find Fred Manton round about now?'

'The Flamingo for sure.'

'Can you get me in the back way? I'd like to give him a surprise.'

'Nothing simpler,' Lazer said. 'He has a private service stair with a door to the alley at the side. You wait there and I can go in the front way and open it for you.'

'Then let's get moving, I'm running out of time,' Garvald said and somewhere in the distance, muffled by the rain and fog, the Town Hall clock sounded the first stroke of midnight.

10

At forty-five, Jack Brady had been a policeman for nearly a quarter of a century. Twenty-five years of working a three-shift system, of being disliked by his neighbours, of being able to spend only one weekend in seven at home with his family and the consequent effect upon his relationship with his son and daughter.

He was not a clever man, but he was patient and possessed the kind of intelligence that can slowly but surely cut through to the heart of things and this, coupled with an extensive knowledge of human nature gained from a thousand long hard Saturday nights on the town and numerous times like them, made him a good policeman.

He had no conscious thought, or even desire, to help society. Society consisted of the civilians who sometimes got mixed up in the constant state of guerrilla warfare that existed between the police and the criminal and, if anything, he preferred the criminal. At least you knew where you were with him.

But he was no sentimentalist. A villain was a villain and there was no such thing as a good thief. One corruption was all corruption. He'd read that somewhere and as he walked through the streets, head down against the rain, he remembered it and thought of Ben Garvald.

From the way he had discussed the case with Grant, Miller had seemed to take a fancy to Garvald. If that was his attitude, then the sooner he fell flat on his face and got the boot, the better. A copper's job was to catch thieves and all the education in the world couldn't teach a man to do that – only experience.

Brady sighed morosely and paused to light a cigarette. The strange thing was that now that his initial anger had evaporated, he found to his surprise that he had been more impressed with Miller than he had thought possible. On the other hand, that was no reason for not teaching him a lesson. It would sharpen the lad up for next time.

Gascoigne Square was a quiet backwater no more than a quarter of a mile from the Town Hall. Its gracious Georgian town houses were still in excellent condition and occupied mainly as offices by solicitors and other professional men, but one or two of the larger houses had proved ideal for conversion into the kind of night club-cum-gaming houses that had mushroomed all over the country since the change in the law.

And some of them also provided for more elemental needs. Brady smiled sardonically as he passed Club Eleven and a taxi unloaded half a dozen middle-aged business men who jostled each other excitedly as they went up the steps to the narrow entrance.

They'd get everything they needed in that hole. Molly Ryan would see to that and one or two of them might even pick up a little more than they'd bargained for. But that was life and you took a chance with each new day that dawned.

The Flamingo certainly had more class, but still looked a little out of character in the old Square with its striped awning and garish neon lighting. A few yards from the entrance, a small wizened man in tweed cap and army greatcoat sat on an orange box, a pile of Sunday newspapers spread out beside him.

The old man knew Brady and Brady knew the old man, but no sign of recognition passed between them. The policeman mounted the steps to the entrance and passed through the glass door that a commissionaire in red uniform held open for him.

A dark haired Italian in a white dinner jacket

moved forward at once, an expression of consternation on his face. He tried to conceal it with a brave smile, but failed miserably.

'Mr Brady. What a pleasure. There is something I can do for you?'

Brady stood there, hands in the pockets of his cheap raincoat, ignoring the man, distaste on his face as he took in the thick carpets, the cream and gold décor and the cloakroom girl in her fishnet stockings.

'I want Manton. Where is he?'

'Is there perhaps something wrong, Mr Brady?'

'There will be if you don't get Manton down here fast.'

A party of three or four people, newly arrived, glanced at him curiously and the Italian stepped to a door marked *Private* and opened it.

'I believe Mr Manton is at the bar. If you'll wait in here, I'll go and see.'

Brady moved inside and the door closed behind him. The office was little more than a cubbyhole, with a desk and a green filing cabinet taking up most of the space. There was a half-completed staff duty list on the blotting pad and he turned it round and examined it idly, noting a familiar name here and there.

The door clicked open behind him and closed again. When Brady turned, Fred Manton was leaning against the door, lighting a cigarette. He was a tall, lean man with good shoulders that showed to advantage in the well-cut dinner jacket. The blue eyes and clipped moustache gave him a faintly military air which went down well with the customers, many of whom nicknamed him the Major and imagined him the product of one of the better public schools.

Nothing could have been further from the truth as Brady knew well and he dropped the duty list on the blotter and looked Manton up and down, contempt and open dislike on his face.

Manton went behind the desk, opened a drawer. He held up the duty list. 'Some people might say you'd been sticking your nose into things that didn't concern you.'

'You're breaking my heart,' Brady said. 'Garvald – Ben Garvald. Where is he?'

Manton seemed genuinely surprised. 'You must be getting old. Last I heard he was in Wandsworth. I thought everybody knew that.'

'He was released yesterday. But you wouldn't know about that, would you?'

Manton shrugged. 'I haven't seen Ben in nine years, not since the day he went down the steps for the Steel Amalgamated job in Birmingham or aren't you familiar with that one?'

'In detail,' Brady said. 'Garvald's wheelman got clear away after that little tickle. We never did manage to run him down.'

'Well, don't look at me,' Manton said. 'I was at home that night.'

'Who said so, your mother?' Brady sneered.

Manton crushed his cigarette in the ashtray very deliberately and reached for the telephone. 'I don't know what you're trying to pull, but I'm getting my lawyer in before I say another word.'

As he lifted the receiver, Brady pulled it from his hand and replaced it in its cradle. 'All right, Manton, let's stop playing games. I want Garvald. Where is he?'

'How should I know, for Christ's sake. This is the last place he'll show, believe me.'

'When we pulled him in for the Steel Amalgamated job, you and he were partners in a club on the other side of the river.'

'That's right. The old One-Spot. So what?'

'Maybe Garvald thinks you still owe him something or did you pay him off while he was inside?'

'Pay him off?' Manton started to laugh. 'What with – washers? After they pulled Ben in, your boys cracked down on the One-Spot so hard we went bust inside a month. I owed money from here to London. So did Ben if it comes to that, but he wasn't around when the bailiffs arrived. I was.'

There was a bitterness in his voice that gave the whole sorry story the stamp of truth and Brady, facing the fact that his hunch had been wrong, swallowed his disappointment and made one last try.

'You've got a place of your own upstairs haven't you? I'd like to have a look round.'

'Got a warrant?'

'What do you think?'

Manton shrugged. 'It doesn't matter. Look all you want. If you find Ben, let me know. I could put him to work for two years and he'd still owe me money.'

'My heart bleeds for you,' Brady said and he opened the door.

Manton smiled, teeth gleaming beneath the clipped moustache. 'Come to think of it, I could do with another man on the door in the spring, Brady. How long before you retire?'

Brady's hand tightened on the door handle, the knuckles whitening as the anger churned up into his throat in a tight ball that threatened to choke him.

He took a deep breath and when he spoke, his voice was remarkably controlled. 'Now that was a stupid remark for a smart boy like you to make, Manton. Really stupid.'

And Manton knew it. As his smile evaporated, Brady grinned gently, closed the door and walked across the thick carpet to the entrance.

The rain, which had drifted on the wind for most of the evening, was falling heavily now and he paused beside the old newspaper man who was swathing himself in a groundsheet. Brady picked up a newspaper and opened it at the sports page.

'Ben Garvald, Micky. Remember him?'

The old man's voice was hoarse and broken, roughened by disease and bad liquor over the years. 'Couldn't forget one like him, Mr Brady.'

'Has he gone in the Flamingo tonight?'

The old man ignored him, pretending to search for change in one of his pockets. 'Not a chance. There's always Manton's private entrance, mind you, beside the staff door in the alley. There's a stair straight up to his flat.'

'Good man, Micky.'

Brady dropped a couple of half crowns into the old man's palm, received a copper or two in change for appearances' sake and moved away. At the corner of the alley which cut along the side of the Flamingo, he paused and glanced back. There was no sign of the commissionaire at the entrance and he moved into the narrow opening quickly.

There was a row of overflowing dustbins, and an old gas lamp bracketed to a wall illuminated two doors. One was marked *Private – Staff Only*. The other carried no sign and when he tried the handle, it was locked.

At the other end of the alley, he could see the main road and the sound of the late night traffic was muted and strange as if it came from another place. He checked his watch. It was a little after eleven and he didn't have to return to the office till midnight. He went back along the alley towards the square, found a doorway, moved into the shadows and waited.

It was bitterly cold and time passed slowly. He leaned in the corner, hands thrust deep into his pockets, and time crawled, minute by slow minute, and no one came. He was wrong, that was the truth of it. *You must be getting old.* Manton had said that and maybe it was true. Was this all he had to show for twenty-five years?

A strange nostalgia gripped him. If only he could start again, go back to the beginning, how different everything would be. As if from a great distance, he seemed to hear voices. He took a deep breath and came back to reality with a start, realizing to his annoyance, that he had almost fallen asleep.

A man had moved from the shadows and stood beside the staff entrance lighting a cigarette. Brady recognized Chuck Lazer at once, and also remembered that the American was employed as a pianist at the club.

As the staff door closed on Lazer, Brady leaned back again, shivering as a cold wind moved along the alley, lifting the skirts of his raincoat. He was wasting his time, that much was obvious.

He lifted his wrist to examine the luminous dial of his watch and saw to his astonishment that it was ten minutes past twelve and at that moment the door to Manton's private staircase opened and someone whistled softly. Ben Garvald moved out of the shadows farther along the alley, paused under the lamp and vanished inside.

Trapped by his own astonishment, Brady stayed there in the shadow for a moment, then pulling himself together, he went forward, a cold finger of excitement making his stomach hollow.

The door to Fred Manton's private staircase was still immovable, but the staff entrance opened to his touch and he hurried inside.

11

When Lazer opened the private door and Garvald entered, he found himself in a small square hall at the bottom of a flight of carpeted stairs. Lazer went first. At the top, he opened a door cautiously and peered into a narrow corridor.

'What have we got here?' Garvald demanded softly.

'Manton's private suite. His office is at the far end. He's in there now, I've just been speaking to him. He wants me to take a couple of boys from the band and go up to Bella's place to make with the mood music. Big party night.'

'Anything special?'

'Harry's birthday.'

'She *must* be getting sentimental in her old age,' Garvald said. 'Don't tell her you've seen me. I'd like it to be a surprise.'

'My pleasure.' Lazer grinned widely. 'Maybe you'll be up there later on?'

'Depends on how the cards fall. I'm staying at the Regent Hotel in Gloyne Street. If anything comes up, you can get in touch with me there.'

'Will do.' They moved along the corridor and the American opened a green baize door on the left. 'This way to hell,' he said as music and laughter drifted up. 'Don't do anything I would.'

Garvald went along the corridor and paused outside the door at the far end. For a moment he hesitated, waiting for some sound through the half-open transom. He was conscious of a movement behind him and turned quickly.

A tall, broad shouldered man was standing watching him. He had long dark hair swept back over each ear, curling slightly at the nape of the neck and one good eye regarded Garvald unwinkingly. The other was coated with an obscene patina of cream and silver.

'What's a game, Jack?' he demanded in a harsh voice.

Garvald looked him up and down calmly, turned without a word and opened the door. The room into which he entered was decorated in cream and gold and a fire flickered in a Queen Anne fireplace. Manton was sitting behind a walnut desk, papers spread before him. He glanced up with a start.

For several moments he and Garvald looked

steadily at each other and then Manton sighed. 'I
hoped you wouldn't do this, Ben.'

'Come back?' Garvald shrugged, opened a silver
box on the desk and helped himself to a cigarette.
'A man needs his friends after what I've been
through, Fred. Where else would I go?'

The man with the wall-eye spoke from the
doorway. 'He couldn't have got in through the
club or the kitchen, Mr Manton, they'd have
buzzed through. That means the side door. Shall I
check him for a key?'

'You do and I'll break your arm,' Garvald said
genially.

Wall-eye took a sudden step forward, his face
dark, and Manton held up a hand. 'Leave it,
Donner. He'd put you in hospital for a month and
I need you around. Go back downstairs.'

Donner stood there for a moment, his single
eye glaring ferociously at Garvald, then he turned
on his heel and the door slammed behind him.

Manton went to a wall cabinet, opened it and
took out a bottle of whisky and two glasses. He
filled them both and toasted Garvald silently.

'How *did* you get in, Ben?'

'Now I ask you,' Garvald said. 'When did I ever
need a key to open a door?'

Manton chuckled. 'That's true enough, God
knows. You were the best door and window man
in the business in the old days.'

He moved back to the desk and lit a cigarette, taking his time over it. 'Why did you come back, Ben? There's nothing for you here.'

'Then why were you so anxious to keep me out? Sicking those two tearaways on to me in the fog outside Wandsworth yesterday was a mistake. Nothing on earth could have kept me away after that.'

'Things have changed,' Manton said. 'It isn't like the old days any more. The kind of money people throw around now, you can make more out of a good legitimate club than we ever did from the rackets. With the form you have behind you, Ben, you'd be bad for business. It's as simple as that.'

'They tell me you work for wages now, I never thought I'd see the day.'

'If you know that, then you know who I work for,' Manton said calmly. 'Harry Faulkner – and he treats me just fine. I get a good basic plus a slice of the cake twice a year. More than we ever dreamed of making at the old One-Spot.'

'When you were in partnership with me.'

Manton put down his glass and said deliberately: 'Let's get one thing straight, Ben. After the coppers picked you up for that Steel Amalgamated job, they shut the One-Spot up tight. It took me two years of working for Faulkner to pay off the debts. I don't owe you a thing.'

Garvald grinned. 'I didn't say you did.'

Manton was unable to control his surprise. He stood behind the desk frowning suspiciously, and then, as if coming to a sudden decision, sat down, took out a bunch of keys and unlocked a drawer. 'Oh, what the hell. So I owe you a favour.' He produced a couple of packets of notes and threw them on to the blotter. 'There's five hundred there, Ben, that's all I can manage.'

Garvald looked down at the money, a strange smile on his face, then he moved to the cabinet and poured himself another whisky. When he turned, his face was without expression.

'No thanks, Fred.'

Manton jumped up angrily. 'Then what do you want? Is it Bella?'

'She *is* my wife, Fred.'

'Don't you mean *was?*' Manton chuckled sourly. 'That kind of talk's going to get you nowhere. Bother her and Harry Faulkner will have you cut down to size so fast you won't know what hit you.'

Garvald smiled. 'And you telling me everything was so legitimate these days.'

Manton frowned, a puzzled expression in his eyes. 'No, it isn't Bella, is it? It's the cash – the cash from that Steel Amalgamated job.'

'Which went up like a torch with Jacky Charlton.'

'Or did it?' Manton said softly. 'Maybe you'd already divvied up?'

'An interesting thought, you must agree.'

There was a rush of footsteps in the corridor, the door was thrown open and Donner came in. He leaned on the desk, ignoring Garvald. 'There's a load of trouble on its way. That blasted copper, Brady.'

'What's he want?'

'Our friend here. Jango's stalling him at the bottom of the stairs, but I wouldn't give him long.'

Manton looked at Garvald angrily. 'What in the hell have you been up to?'

The big Irishman was already on his way to the door. 'Search me, but I've got other fish to fry. Give him my respects, Fred. I'll see myself out.'

As he disappeared along the corridor, Donner moved to go after him, but Manton caught him by the sleeve. 'Let him go. He hasn't been here, understand?'

He sat down behind his desk and lit a cigarette. A moment later, he heard voices in the corridor and Brady burst into the room, brushing aside a small, black-bearded man in a dinner jacket, whose black hair was close-cropped to his skull.

He stood at the side of Manton's desk, his face swollen with passion, and spoke with a heavy Greek accent. 'He came in through the staff entrance like a crazy man, boss,' he said, one hand weaving an intricate pattern in front of Manton's face. 'When I tried to stop him coming up, he nearly broke my arm.'

'Never mind this little squirt,' Brady said harshly. 'I want Ben Garvald. Where is he?'

Manton managed a frown with little difficulty. 'Ben Garvald? You must be out of your tiny mind.'

Brady went round the desk in a rush and jerked Manton to his feet, one massive hand crushing the silken lapels of the expensive dinner jacket. 'Don't give me that kind of crap, Manton, I was outside in the alley. Someone let him in through your private door.'

For a second only, Manton lost control. He glanced at Donner with a frown and Brady laughed harshly. 'I read you like a book, you pig. Now where is he?'

Manton pulled himself free and backed away. 'I don't know what all this is about, but I'd like to see your warrant. If you haven't got one you'd better get to hell out of here before I call in some real law.'

'You don't frighten me,' Brady said contemptuously.

'Maybe not,' Manton told him, 'but Harry Faulkner will.'

But Brady had already passed over into that area where action is in command of reason. At the best of times, caution had never been one of his virtues.

He glared at Manton, his eyes bloodshot. 'Ben

Garvald's here, I saw him come in and, by God, I'm going to find him.'

He swung round, shoved Jango to one side with a careless sweep of his arm and went into the corridor. He opened the first door on the left, switched on the light and found himself in the bathroom.

When he turned to walk out, the three men were standing in the corridor watching him. There was a slight, polite smile on Manton's face. 'Find anything?'

'Maybe he thinks we flushed Garvald away,' Donner said.

Brady ignored both remarks and opened the next door.

'The sitting room,' Manton said helpfully. 'My bedroom next to it.'

Brady checked both of them without success and as he came out of the bedroom, noticed that a door at the other end of the corridor was standing slightly ajar. He moved to it quickly, pulled it open and looked down the stairs to Manton's private entrance.

He turned, his face suffused with passion. 'So that's it.'

'For Christ's sake, boss, how long is this farce running for?' Donner said, turning to Manton. 'Can't you give him a couple of fivers or something? Maybe that's all he came for in the first place.'

A growl of anger erupted from Brady's throat and he grabbed at Donner's shoulder, pulling him round. All Donner's pent-up rage and frustration surged out of him like a dam bursting.

'You keep your bloody paws off me,' he said viciously. He turned, catching the punch that Brady flung at him on his left shoulder and, at the same moment, moved in close, raising a knee into the unprotected groin. As Brady doubled over, the knee swung into his face, lifting him back. For a movement, the big policeman poised there in the doorway, clawing at the wall for support and then he went backwards into the dark well of the staircase.

12

As the three men stood in shocked silence, crowding the doorway, there was a slight creak behind them and Ben Garvald emerged from the linen cupboard.

'You're getting careless in your old age, Fred.' He shook his head. 'Remember the eleventh commandment? Never do a copper for it shall be returned unto you an hundredfold.'

He brushed past them and went down the stairs. Brady was lying on his back at the bottom, legs sprawled in an unnatural position on the stairs, head and shoulders jammed against the wall. Blood matted his hair, trickling down into his eyes and his head moved slightly.

Garvald turned and looked up at Manton who had paused six or seven steps from the bottom. 'He doesn't look too good, Fred. I wish you joy.'

He opened the door and went out in one quick motion. As it closed, Manton pulled Jango down beside him. 'Get after him. Lose him and I'll have your ears.'

The door opened and closed behind the Cypriot and Manton dropped to one knee beside Brady. The policeman opened his eyes and glared up at him. There was a strange, choking sound in his throat, blood trickled from his nostrils and his head lolled to one side.

'My God, he's croaked,' Donner said in a whisper.

Manton got to his feet. 'What a bloody mess.'

'It was an accident,' Donner said desperately. 'He swung at me first. You saw.'

'I can just see a judge and jury taking my word for that,' Manton said bitterly. 'Be your age, Donner. You've killed a copper and that's a topping job.'

Donner pointed a shaking finger at him. 'If I go, you go. We're in this together, make no mistake about that.'

'You don't need to rub it in,' Manton said. 'Even if those swine up at the Town Hall couldn't find any evidence to implicate me, they'd invent some.'

'Then we've got to get rid of him,' Donner said. 'That stands to reason. What about dumping him in the canal off Grainger's Wharf? That's not far away.'

'That would make it look more like murder than ever,' Manton said. 'It's got to be cleverer than that. An accident, that's what we want. A convenient accident. Hit and run, perhaps.'

Donner nodded eagerly. 'That's not bad. That's not bad at all.'

'Especially if we used someone else's car and dumped it later. There's one thing, though. Who else saw him come in?'

'Only Jango,' Donner said 'Luckily it was the staff break before the main floor show. They were all in the kitchen. He kept Brady talking at the bottom of the stairs and buzzed for me.' He hesitated. 'There's always Garvald.'

'We'll see to him later. First, we've got to get rid of our friend here. We'll take him up the alley between us to Stank's Yard, then you go and pick up a car and don't waste any time.'

The alley was deserted and they moved through the darkness, Brady's limp body a dead weight between them. Stank's Yard was at the far end near the main road and the door to it from the alley was never kept locked.

It was a dark well of a place between tall warehouses due for demolition. Much used by scrap merchants, it was choked with the accumulated junk of the years. Wide gates giving access to a narrow lane leading into the main road stood permanently open.

Manton leaned against the wall, trying to shelter from the driving rain, a cigarette cupped in one hand. Strangely enough, he wasn't afraid. Excited, if anything. In a strange way it was as if he were living again for the first time in years and he grinned ruefully. Now that would have given Ben Garvald a laugh if you like.

Someone entered the alley behind him from the main road and moved quickly along the uneven flag-stones, footsteps echoing between the high brick walls. Manton stood back and waited. A moment later, Jango passed the doorway, his face clear in the dim light of the gas lamp which hung at the entrance to the alley.

Manton called softly to him and Jango turned and came hurrying back. He peered cautiously through the darkness. 'What's going on?'

'Brady died on us. We've got to get rid of him. I'm waiting for Donner to show up with a car.'

The Cypriot's breath whistled between his teeth. 'That isn't so good, Mr Manton. I'm not so sure I like to be mixed up in a killing.'

'You're in it up to your neck whether you like it or not,' Manton told him brutally. 'Unless you'd like me to remind someone about all that killing you did for EOKA. Now cut out the double talk and tell me about Garvald.'

'He's staying at a place called the Regent Hotel in Gloyne Street. It's no more than five minutes' walk from here. A fleapit. They don't even have a night porter on duty, just a chambermaid.'

'Did you speak to her?'

'Sure.' Jango chuckled and his eyes gleamed through the darkness. 'She's a whore, Mr Manton. I know that place. They only keep her on to oblige the customers. A pound in the top of her stocking and she'll give you fifty-seven varieties.'

'How interesting,' Manton said softly. 'And just how far would she be willing to go for twenty quid?'

'I shudder all over to think of it,' Jango said simply.

The sudden roar of an engine echoed within the narrow walls and twin headlamps picked them out of the darkness as a vehicle moved in through the main gates.

It was a blue Thames van and as they went forward Donner got out of the driving seat. 'Best I could do. Get him in the back and let's get out of here.'

There was still light traffic about, but the lateness of the hour and the heavy, constant rain had by now almost cleared the streets as Donner drove out of the yard and turned into the main road.

'Don't waste time on anything fancy,' Manton told him. 'Any of these side streets will do.'

'Maybe it's not so good to make it so near the club,' Jango said.

'Use your brains,' Manton told him. 'He works

Central Division, doesn't he, and he was seen to call at the club earlier on. It's got to be round here.'

Donner swung the wheel, crossing the dual carriageway, and turned into a narrow street that swung in a curve between tall warehouses towards the river. By now, it was raining even harder and the unheated cab was bitterly cold.

'This should do it,' Donner said and he braked in the middle of the deserted street so that the Thames skidded on the wet asphalt.

Manton opened the door and jumped out. The street had started to curve and at this point they were out of sight of the main road and the warehouses, lifting into the night on either side, were dark and still.

'Keep the engine running,' he told Donner. 'Jango and I can handle this.'

He moved to the rear of the van, opened the doors and pulled Brady out by the ankles. The Cypriot took him by the shoulders and together they carried him round to the front of the van, and propped the body upright against the bonnet.

They stood back and allowed Brady to slide to the ground, the blood that had soaked his face and shirt leaving its traces on the bonnet of the van. Manton raised his foot and smashed the near-side headlamp, glass splintering in a shower that cascaded over Brady's crumpled body.

'That should do it,' he said and clambered into the van, pushing Jango in ahead of him.

'Maybe I should run over him or something,' Donner said. 'Just to make it look good.'

As Manton hesitated, for the suggestion had its merits, the light from a car's headlamps splayed against the curved wall of a warehouse in front of them.

'Get moving,' he said hoarsely.

Donner slammed the van into reverse and the rear wheels bounced over the kerb as he swung the wheel. They shot forward, one wheel bumping over Brady's right foot, and drove away quickly as a small saloon car came round the curve behind them.

'I don't want it any closer than that,' Donner said as they crossed the dual carriageway into another side street.

'What do we do now?'

'You can drop Jango and me on the next corner,' Manton said. 'Then turn into Canal Street and run this thing off Grainger's Wharf. We don't want to make it too easy for them. We'll see you back at the club and make it fast. There's Garvald to take care of, remember.'

'Now that I look forward to,' Donner said. 'I really do.'

The man at the wheel of the saloon car was past his prime and the girl in the passenger seat was certainly not his wife, an added complication. He looked across in fascinated horror at the body which sprawled in the middle of the road and glanced nervously at the shadows crowding from the warehouse walls.

'The rotten swine,' the girl said. 'Didn't even stop.'

Her companion nodded, opened the door and walked across to Brady. When he came back he looked sick.

'Blood all over his face, I think he's dead.'

'Then we'd better get out of here,' the girl said briskly.

He turned, horror in his eyes. 'We can't just leave him here.'

'Why not?' she said brutally. 'We certainly can't do him any good. If it makes you feel any better, we can stop at the first call box. Dial 999, but don't give your name.' He sat there staring at her and she shrugged. 'Of course, if you want to see your name in the paper . . .

It was all he needed. He switched on the motor and drove away quickly, leaving the horror behind him under the dim light of the old-fashioned gas lamp.

After a while, the body stirred and a strange, inhuman sob lifted in the throat. Jack Brady rolled on to his face and tried to push himself up, but the arm was broken and he slumped forward, his blood washing across the asphalt, waiting for them to come as he knew they would, hanging on to that final hidden reserve that is in all men and which refused to allow him to die.

The bell of the approaching patrol car, a cry in the night, was warm and comforting and it was only when he heard it that he let go and slid into darkness again.

Ben Garvald lay on the bed smoking a cigarette and stared up at the ceiling. He'd had a lot of practice over the years, but this was different. Here, he could walk out any time he felt like it.

He wondered what Manton was doing about the copper and a grin touched the corners of his mouth. Now there was a problem, but on the other hand, no skin off his nose. He checked his watch. It was 1 a.m. and he frowned, trying to plan ahead.

If it was the sort of party he imagined it would be, it could run till morning. Certainly there was no point in trying to contact Bella before four or five by which time most of her guests would probably either be flat on their backs or in no fit state to know what was going on. He smiled, trying to imagine the look on her face when she first saw him.

There was a light knock on the door, it opened and the Irish girl came in with a cup and saucer in one hand. 'I made some tea.'

'I'll remember you in my prayers.'

She gave him the tea and laughed as she looked down at him. 'That'll be the day.'

She went to the window and stood looking into the street. When he had finished his tea, she came back and sat on the edge of the bed.

'Mind if I have a cigarette?'

'Help yourself.'

She took one and he produced his lighter. When she leaned forward, the nylon overall opened to the waist. She was wearing a slip, no brassière and her breasts were white and firm. She held his wrist tightly as she lit her cigarette, looking straight into his eyes. Garvald slid his left hand inside the neck of the overall and cupped it over a breast, the nipple hardening immediately against his palm.

'Aren't you the one?' she said softly.

He dropped the lighter, took the cigarette from her mouth and crushed it into the ashtray on the bedside table. 'It's been a long time,' he said. 'A hell of a long time. I'm warning you.'

Her arms went around his neck and he slid the overall down over her shoulders as their mouths came together. He was trembling, just like a kid having it for the first time, which was strange, and the light in the room seemed to grow dimmer.

She tumbled on to her back, her limbs asprawl, pulling him down into her softness, but his body seemed to have turned to water. For some reason he was on the floor and she was sitting on the edge of the bed staring down at him, the overall rucked up around her thighs, and her legs were the longest and most beautiful things he had ever seen.

Across the bed, the door opened and Donner came in. He was laughing but there was also something else in his face and when his mouth opened no sound seemed to come out. He moved round the end of the bed and Garvald tried to haul himself up, but it was too late. A boot swung into his side and the girl's cry was the last thing he heard as he plunged into the dark.

13

Nick lit a cigarette and sat on the edge of the table and watched her. After a while, Wilma emptied her glass with a shudder. She looked up at him, eyes wide and staring, the mascara smudged by her tears.

'I must look like hell. Could I have another?'

'It's your gin.'

He reached for the bottle and half filled her glass. 'Things must be pretty bad when you try to go out like that.'

She took the gin down in one quick swallow, made a face and reached for the bottle again. 'I thought you were my husband.'

'You must think the world of him.'

'I wouldn't cut him down if he was hanging.' She laughed harshly. 'I'll tell you about my husband, mister. I'll tell you all there is to know about Sammy Rosco. He's from under a stone.

When he picked me off a Hamburg street in 1945 and married me, I thought it was a miracle. In those days I still prayed. I was only fifteen, but I lied about my age.'

'What happened?'

'We came home when he got demobbed. Home to this place.' She looked around her, an expression of loathing on her face.

'The honeymoon lasted for as long as it took him to run through his gratuity, then he brought the first man home.'

'And he's lived off you ever since?'

'Something like that. Come one, come all, drunk or sober, black or white, I was never known to refuse. Sammy saw to that. The first time I tried, he knocked me senseless. Roses all the way.'

'Ever tried moving out?'

'You could say that.' She emptied her glass and ran a hand over her eyes. 'Look, I've got a train to catch. I don't know who gave you my address, but I'm not playing those kind of games any more.'

'I didn't come for that.'

She hadn't eaten since lunch and the gin had gone straight to her head so that when she looked up at him, she had to concentrate hard, a frown on her face.

'Who are you?' And then in alarm, 'You aren't a friend of Sammy's, are you?'

'Not from the sound of him,' Nick said and

took a chance. 'Nick Miller's the name. I'm a pal of Ben Garvald's.'

'You're a friend of Ben's?' She peered up at him in bewilderment. 'Come to think of it, I have seen you somewhere before,' and for some unaccountable reason she shivered.

'You couldn't have,' Nick told her. 'I'm new in town. Ben and I did some bird together at Parkhurst. I was released last October.'

'You've just missed him,' she said. 'He was here a little while ago.'

'I was supposed to meet him outside Wandsworth yesterday, but something came up. I hear there was trouble.'

'They were waiting for him in the fog,' she said, staring into her empty glass.

Nick filled it again quickly. 'Who was, Wilma?'

'Oh, some rat or other that Sammy knew on the inside.' She started to laugh and drank some more of the gin. 'My God, he couldn't have told them much about Ben.'

'He's a hard man all right.'

'He can take 'em all.' She stared dreamily into space. 'But when it comes to women.' She shook her head drunkenly, slow tears oozing down her cheeks and reached for her handbag. 'See this?' She waved the fifty pounds in Nick's face. 'That's Ben for you. I'm going home, do you understand? I'm going home.'

'What about Sammy?'

She laughed contemptuously. 'Ben gave him the hiding of his life, then tossed him out on his ear.'

'Good for Ben.' Nick walked to the fireplace and kept his back to her.

'One thing I don't understand. Why would Sammy want to have Ben worked over when he came out of Wandsworth yesterday? It doesn't make any kind of sense.'

'You don't think he was working for himself, do you?' She stopped abruptly, as she caught sight of his face in the mirror over the fireplace.

'Go on, Wilma,' Nick said turning. 'Who was he working for?'

A sudden realization came to her that something was wrong and she shook her head vigorously and got to her feet.

'I don't know, I don't remember. I've got to get out of here. I've a train to catch.'

She reached for her case, but Nick beat her to it. 'Was it Fred Manton?'

She stared up at him, sobering rapidly, a dawning comprehension in her eyes. 'You aren't any friend of Ben's.'

She came closer, peering up into his face and Nick nodded slowly. 'Right every time, Wilma. I'm the law.'

There was real horror in her eyes now and she sobered completely, grabbing for the case and trying to push past him. 'I've done nothing wrong. You can't hold me here. I've got a train to catch.'

Nick shoved her back with all his force. 'Where did Ben go, Wilma? Tell me that and I'll run you to the station myself.'

For a moment she seemed to have lost the power of speech and then she pointed a shaking finger at him and the words came tumbling out.

'I know now why I was afraid of you, where I've seen you before. When I was a kid in Hamburg during the war, I had a cousin just like you, same white face, same eyes that looked through you like glass. He was in the Gestapo. When the end came, a mob hung him from a lamp post at the end of our street.'

'Ben,' Nick said. 'Where is he, Wilma? I only want a chat with him. He's done nothing wrong, yet.'

'You could put a white-hot poker on my feet and I wouldn't tell you. He's the only man ever treated me like a human being in my life.'

Nick shrugged. 'That's too bad. That means I'll have to take you in for questioning. You'll miss your train.'

Her face went very white, the mouth slack and she stared stupidly at him. 'But if I miss my train, Sammy will catch up with me again. He'll bring me back.'

Her head moved slowly from side to side and

Nick said patiently, 'All you have to do is tell me where Ben was going when he left here.'

The strange thing was that she genuinely didn't know and yet an inner pride, a strength she had never realized she possessed before, refused to allow her to betray the man who had helped her.

She swallowed the tears and her chin tilted. 'All right, so we go to the station.'

Nick sighed heavily and nodded. 'That's right, Wilma. The railway station. Come on. I'll give you a lift in my car.'

She stared at him incredulously, then snatched up her case and pushed round him. 'I'd rather ride with the devil.'

He followed her along the dark passage, down the steps into the yard and reached for her shoulder as she turned into the street beside his car.

'Don't be a fool, Wilma. I can have you there in a couple of minutes. There's a train at twelve twenty. We'll just make it.'

'Take your hands off me.' She pulled away. 'From now on, I walk alone.' Her face was yellow in the lamplight and full of hate as she gazed up at him. 'English police, Gestapo, what's the difference? You don't give a damn who gets hurt as long as you find out what you want to know. I hope Ben Garvald cracks your skull.'

She spat on the pavement at his feet, turned and walked away, the case banging against her leg, her high heels clicking on the hollow pavement, fading into the night. Nick stood there gazing into the darkness. After a while, he got back into the Mini-Cooper and drove away.

He ran from the car and mounted the steps to the plain white door that was the entrance to Club Eleven, head down against the driving rain. He pressed the bell and looked along the wet pavement to the Flamingo, a bright splash of light in the darkness. That could come later. For the moment, there was nothing he wanted so much as a few quiet words with Sammy Rosco.

The door opened and he moved in past a uniformed commissionaire and found himself standing in a tiny, thickly carpeted foyer. A young girl in black stockings and not much else, took his coat and a white-haired military-looking type came forward and smiled charmingly.

'Membership card, sir?'

'I haven't got one, but I'd like to see Miss Ryan. Tell her it's Nick Miller.'

'A personal friend, sir?'

'I think you could say that. We've even pounded the same beat together.' The man frowned and Nick produced his warrant card and dropped it on to the reception desk. 'Give her this with my compliments.'

The man's face fell, but he picked up the

telephone and pressed a button. After a few moments' muttered conversation he replaced the receiver. When he turned, the smile was back and pasted firmly into place.

'Miss Ryan will be with you in just a moment, Mr Miller. Perhaps you would care to wait at the bar? The floor show is just beginning.'

'I'll find my own way,' Nick said.

He went through a door at the end of the passage and found himself standing at the top of a short flight of steps which dropped into a crowded dining-room. Above the tables was a raised catwalk and scantily dressed show girls were engaged in a dance routine.

The tables were crowded and the customers were exclusively men, most of them being entertained by the hostesses Club Eleven supplied in such profusion.

Nick ordered a drink and stood at the end of the crowded bar. After a while, there was a drum roll and a fat and balding comedian came skipping along the catwalk, a mike in one hand.

His patter was the usual mixture of crude filth and innuendo, but mixed in with it was a genuine acid wit, mostly directed at the customers themselves, a fact none of them seemed to grasp.

Finally the comedian stood to one side and took up his ancillary role as compère of the big event of the evening and the one for which, to judge from the applause, most of the customers had been waiting.

It was the usual sort of thing. Famous beauties through the ages. Each time the comedian announced a name, a curtain rose at the back of the room disclosing a nude tableau and various fleshy young women depicting Helen of Troy, Eve in the Garden and so on.

At various times, the girls paraded along the catwalk, displaying their ample charms in a manner the Lord Chamberlain would have found very difficult to accept. All the time, the comedian kept up a line of patter that verged on the obscene.

There was sweat on the faces at the tables in the half light beneath the catwalk, lust and desire and grasping hands that reached up to touch the legs of the girls parading above.

Finally, there was a sudden gasp as a completely naked coloured girl appeared from behind the curtains and started a slow, careful promenade that reduced the room to silence and awe. She half turned, the room was plunged into darkness and a light bulb flashed between her ample buttocks.

'Ten thousand volts,' the comedian cried and as the lights came on again, the room rocked with laughter.

Nick turned to reach for his drink and found Molly standing a few feet away looking at him. She was somewhere in her late twenties, a striking redhead in a green dress that showed off to advantage a figure that was still worth looking at. There was strength in her face, a touch of arrogance, but when she looked at Nick and smiled, there was nothing but warmth there.

'It's been a long time, Nick.'

'Too long.' He took her hands and held them tightly for a moment. 'I've been away for a year – on a course.'

'So I heard. Detective Sergeant now they tell me.'

'That's right. With Central Division. Let me buy you a drink.'

She shook her head. 'Not here. This is strictly for the mugs and that goes for the kind of booze we sell them too. Let's go up to my office.'

She threaded her way between the tables, dropping a word here and there, mounted a few steps beside the stage and went through a door marked *Private*. Inside, they passed what were obviously the girls' dressing-rooms, and finally came to another door which opened into a small and rather severely furnished room with filing cabinets, a desk and several telephones.

Molly opened a cabinet, took out a bottle of whisky and filled a glass. She handed it to him with a slight smile. 'Irish, pot distilled. I remember what you like.'

'Aren't you having one?'

'Straight poison. I'll never have another drink as long as I live.' She grinned. 'Besides, it slows you down.'

He looked around the room curiously and shook his head. 'Somehow this doesn't seem you.'

'This is my office,' she said calmly and sat down in the chair behind the desk. 'Strictly business. Isn't that what you're here for?'

'You must read me like a book.'

'I should be able to. I've known you long enough.' She chuckled. 'Remember when we first met? You were a young probationer pounding a pavement and I was a probationer of another sort.'

'Two o'clock in the morning and raining cats and dogs.'

'And we'd both had enough, so I took you back to my place.' She laughed. 'You thought I was the original scarlet woman.'

He shook his head. 'Never that, Molly. Never that.'

She lit a cigarette and leaned back in her chair. 'What do you want, Nick?'

'Ben Garvald for a start. Have you seen him tonight?'

She seemed genuinely amazed. 'Have I seen Ben? As far as I know, he's still doing time.'

'Not any more. Got out yesterday. The word is he's back and looking for Bella.'

Molly laughed harshly. 'Then I hope he finds her.'

123

'You don't like her much?'

'She isn't fit to clean his shoes. In my book, he's the tops. Oh, he's hard – hard as steel, but where women are concerned . . .

She sighed, her face softening, and Nick said: 'So you're on his side?'

'I should say so. When I first came over from Ireland, I was a green kid of eighteen. Didn't know the form. Before I knew where I was, the wrong mob had me under their thumb and I was being squeezed dry. Ben Garvald got me out of that, free, gratis and for nothing. That's his one weakness – he can't resist helping a woman in trouble.'

'All right,' Nick said. 'So you haven't seen him tonight?'

'All it happens, I haven't. Has Bella made a complaint?'

'Something like that.'

'The cow. I know where I'd like to see her.'

Nick decided to try another line. 'Is Sammy Rosco here by any chance?'

She nodded. 'He's on duty upstairs. Don't tell me you're looking for him as well?'

'Just a couple of questions. Routine mainly. Can we go up?'

She shrugged. 'I don't see why not.'

They left the office, moved along the passage and paused outside a door which carried the legend *Health Club Section – Members Only.*

'A new name for it,' Nick said, but she ignored the remark, opened the door and led the way in.

They moved along a quiet corridor, passed through a swing door and entered a long tiled room thick with steam. A fat and rather ugly middle-aged man came towards them, swathed in Turkish towels, a young woman in a white nylon smock helping him along. They moved into a cubicle and she pulled the curtain.

The room was lined with such cubicles and one of them didn't have its curtain properly drawn. As Nick passed, he glanced in and saw another fat and ageing specimen lying on a couch while a young woman massaged him. She seemed to find a pair of black knickers sufficient garment in the great heat.

As Molly held open the door at the end for him, she smiled. 'Strictly legal, Nick. They've all got diplomas from an institute of physical culture and massage I know in London.'

'Some institute.'

The room into which they entered was white tiled with a shower stall in one corner and a padded table in the centre. Sammy Rosco was sitting on a chair in the corner reading a magazine. He wore a white singlet and slacks.

'Very ornamental,' Nick said. 'What's he supposed to be?'

Rosco looked up with a frown, then threw down

the magazine and got to his feet. 'Who's the funny man, Molly?'

Nick turned to her quickly. 'You can leave us now.'

'Heh, wait a minute,' she said in surprise.

'I said leave us.' His voice was hard and with the cutting edge of a razor. She turned and went out almost immediately, her face red, and Nick produced his warrant card. 'I haven't got much time, so let's have some straight answers, Rosco. You hired two men to attack Ben Garvald outside Wandsworth yesterday morning. Why?'

Rosco looked over his shoulder like a hunted animal. 'I don't know what you're talking about.'

'Don't waste my time,' Nick said wearily. 'I've seen your wife. She told me what happened at your place earlier and what Ben Garvald did to you.' He poked a finger at the livid bruise on the other man's left cheek. 'He must be quite a puncher.'

'That lousy rotten bitch. Just wait till I get my hands on her. I'll make her wish she'd never been born.'

'You'll have to wait a long time,' Nick said. 'She caught a London train about ten minutes ago. I put her on it myself.' He smiled softly. 'She's gone home, Sammy.'

Rosco shook his head in bewilderment. 'She couldn't. She didn't have the cash.'

'Garvald saw to that. Good of him, wasn't it?'

With a cry of anger and frustration, Rosco swung a tremendous punch, that Nick found no difficulty whatever in avoiding. Remembering Wilma, he moved in fast, his left sank in well below the belt, and his right swung to meet the descending face, splintering teeth. Rosco staggered back, cannoned into the padded table and slid to the tiled floor.

He lay there moaning, blood trickling into his white singlet and Nick crouched beside him. 'That was from Wilma, Sammy. And don't let's have any of that assault by a police officer crap. It wouldn't get you anywhere, believe me. Not with the kind of form you've got behind you.'

As he got to his feet, the door opened and Molly came in. 'He slipped and fell,' Nick said. 'Better see if there's a doctor in the house.'

She looked straight at him, her eyes hard. 'Don't come back, Nick. Never again as a friend. I like to know where I stand.'

'What's this?' he said. 'The Berlin Wall? Me on one side, you on the other?'

'Something like that.'

'Suit yourself. See you sometime.'

He brushed past her and went out through the steam, past the cubicles and into the corridor beyond, his feet sinking into the thick carpet. Strangely enough, he felt no regret. In fact, already his mind was on his next move.

* * *

It was curiosity more than anything else that took him up the steps of the Flamingo. Manton would certainly deny having had any part in the attack on Garvald outside Wandsworth. Would probably deny having seen Garvald even if he had. Still, it might be worth having a look at him.

Manton was in the bedroom of his private suite, hurriedly changing out of his wet clothes, when the phone rang. He listened to what the man on the door had to say and nodded.

'Put him in the front office. I'll be five minutes.'

He dressed quickly in a clean white shirt and dark lounge suit, his mind racing. Detective Sergeant Miller? A new boy. Certainly no one he'd ever heard of round Central Division. But what did he want, that was the thing? The one comforting thought he carried with him when he left the room was that it couldn't have anything to do with Brady – there simply hadn't been enough time.

Nick was examining a framed historical map of the North of England on the wall when Manton came in and he turned and smiled pleasantly.

'Mr Manton – sorry to trouble you, sir. My name's Miller. Detective Sergeant, Central Division. I'm trying to locate an old acquaintance of yours, Ben Garvald. I've reason to believe he arrived in town today and I thought he might have contacted you.'

Manton decided to play the honest but puzzled businessman. 'Everybody wants Ben Garvald. What is all this, Sergeant? As I told Mr Brady earlier I didn't even know Ben was out.'

Nick frowned. 'Jack Brady's been here?'

'About an hour or so ago.' Manton hesitated. 'I hope I haven't said anything out of turn, but he came in through the front door just like you. Everybody saw him.'

'That's all right, Mr Manton,' Nick said. 'A misunderstanding, that's all. So you can't help me with Ben?'

'As I told Brady, I didn't even know he was out.'

'Fair enough. I won't trouble you any more then.' Nick moved to the door, hesitated and turned. 'Just one more thing. Does Sammy Rosco work for you?'

Manton frowned. 'That's right, just along the street from here. Why, what's Sammy been up to?'

'Nothing really,' Nick said pleasantly. 'But I'd get rid of him if I were you.'

'Why should I do that?'

'He tells lies, Mr Manton, mainly about you.'

Nick smiled and the door closed behind him. Manton stood there behind the desk for a moment, eyes narrowed, and then he picked up the telephone and dialled a number.

14

Harry Faulkner's house was in St Martin's Wood, an exclusive residential area not far from Nick's own home. It was a late Victorian mansion set back from the road in a couple of acres of ground. The whole place was a blaze of lights and there were so many cars in the drive he found difficulty in parking.

He mounted the wide steps to the porch and rang the front door bell, but there was no reply. After a while, he tried the ornate bronze handle. The door opened to his touch and he went inside.

The house seemed to be full of people. The hall was crowded with them and couples sat all the way up the stairs, most of them with glasses in their hands.

And every bed occupied, he thought to himself wryly.

He took off his cap and coat, left them on a

walking stick rack in the porch and pushed his way through the crowd towards the sound of a driving piano with rhythm and bass accompaniment that was somehow familiar.

He found himself in the entrance to a long, narrow room flanked by French windows to the terrace outside.

It had a beautifully polished parquet floor, obviously specially laid for dancing and was as crowded as the hall outside.

Chuck Lazer sat at a baby grand in a corner opposite the bar at the far end. Nick was just about to push his way towards him, when he felt a tap on the shoulder and turned quickly.

A tall, heavily built man in his thirties faced him, a polite smile on his face. He wore a dinner jacket that had been cut by someone who knew what he was doing, but the slightly crooked line of the nose and the hard eyes made Nick immediately wary.

'I saw you come in, sir. Is there something I can do for you?'

'And who might you be?'

'Craig, sir. Mr Faulkner's manservant.'

Nick almost laughed out loud. 'I'd like to see Mrs Faulkner. Do you know where she is?'

'She's rather busy right now, sir. Was it something important?'

Nick took out his warrant card. 'I think you'll

find she'll come running when you tell her who
it is.'

The smile disappeared, the eyes seemed harder
than ever. 'If you'd come this way.'

Nick followed him through the crowd along the
hall. Craig paused outside a door, took a key from
his pocket and opened it. 'Mr Faulkner's study,
Sergeant. If you'll wait in here, I'll fetch Mrs
Faulkner. I believe she's in the kitchen checking on
the supper.'

It was a pleasant room, lined with books from
floor to ceiling. There was a magnificent walnut
desk near the Adam fireplace and a small bar in
one corner, carefully designed to stay in character.
From the heavy velvet curtains, to the Persian
carpet on the floor, everything was perfect. Too
perfect. It was as if someone had called in a firm
of interior decorators and ordered a gentleman's
study as per the catalogue.

He helped himself to a cigarette from a box
containing Turkish and Virginian, another anach-
ronism, and moved across to the shelves. From
their general appearance, the books had come with
the study in some kind of package deal. He took
one down, examined it and smiled. Even the pages
hadn't been cut. As he replaced it, the door opened
and Bella came in.

It was quite incredible. She didn't look a day
older, no different from the healthy young animal

he'd worshipped as a kid, hanging around on the corner of Khyber Street to see her go by.

The clothes were more expensive, of course. The red dress had obviously cost Faulkner a packet, the diamond brooch on one shoulder looked real.

But these were inessentials. The hair was still as dark, the eyes bright, mouth full and generous and when she moved to meet him, the old indefinable something was still there. A complete, deep sensuality that would still move men when her hair was grey.

'Miller?' she said. 'Nick Miller? Don't I know you?'

'A long time ago,' he said. 'Around the corner from your old house in Khyber Street. My mother kept a shop.'

Her smile was like a bubble breaking through to the surface. 'Now I remember. You're Phil Miller's kid brother. I met him at a party the other week. He told me all about you.'

'I'm surprised he mentioned me in company.'

She took a cigarette from the box and he gave her a light. 'So you're a Detective Sergeant now?' She shook her head. 'And everywhere I go I see another of those television shops of Phil's. It doesn't make sense. Why aren't you working with him?'

'Phil has a flair for making money.' Nick smiled. 'I run to darker talents. In any case, I'm a sleeping partner.'

'Isn't that illegal or something? For a policeman, I mean?'

'We don't mention that.' He threw his cigarette into the fire. 'I've been trying to run Ben to earth for the past two or three hours without success. He's here in town, but that's as far as I've got.'

'Ben?' she said warily, her smile vanishing. 'What are you talking about?'

'Your sister made a complaint earlier this evening. Said you'd had a message from Ben saying he'd look you up. She asked us to run him down. Warn him not to bother you.'

'Why can't she mind her own damned business?' Bella said angrily.

'I didn't see her personally,' Nick said. 'But from all accounts, she was worried about you. About what might happen if Ben showed up.'

'Worried about herself and that precious school of hers more likely,' Bella flashed back at him, lapsing momentarily into the harsher accent of her youth and then she seemed to pull up short. 'No, that isn't really fair. She does worry about me – always has.' She smiled and shook her head. 'Daft, when you think about it. She's five years younger than me, but she started to do the thinking for both of us a long time ago.'

'Can I see the letter?'

'I've got it in a drawer in the bedroom. I'll only be a second.'

She crossed to the only other door in the room, opened it and went in. Nick could see a luxuriously furnished bedroom in red and gold with a reproduction four-poster bed. She opened a drawer in a dressing-table and came back carrying the letter. It was a small sheet of official prison notepaper, folded to envelope size and dated a couple of days previously. It was brief and to the point. *See you soon – Ben.* Even the prison officer who censored mail could have taken no exception to such an innocent sounding message.

'When did you get this?'

'The day before yesterday.'

'And you haven't shown it to your husband?'

'With his temper?' She shook her head and tapped her fingers impatiently on the edge of the desk. 'What would be the point? It might never happen. If he does show up, it'll be more for old times' sake than anything else. Ben would never do anything to hurt me.'

'Then what are you worrying about?'

She laughed. 'It seems to be Jean who's doing all the worrying. Maybe you'd better have a chat with her.'

'I'd like that.'

'I'll see if I can find her. She may still be in the kitchen. She was giving me a hand with the supper arrangements. You can't trust these catering people out of your sight.'

The door closed behind her and Nick moved across to the fireplace. He was standing with one foot on the polished brass fender, gazing into the flames and thinking about Ben Garvald, when the door opened again.

Some things can happen in life which have such a devastating effect that, after them, nothing can ever be quite the same again. Nick Miller was caught in such a timeless moment when he turned to find Jean Fleming standing just inside the door.

She wore high-heeled shoes, dark stockings, a simple dress of black silk which was barely knee-length and left her arms bare. There was about her a tremendous quality of repose, of detachment, as she stood there looking across at him.

It was as if in some strange way she was waiting for something. It was not that she was beautiful. The dark hair, razor-cut to the skull, gave her a rather boyish appearance and the sallow, Irish peasant face indicated strength more than any other quality, yet never before in his life had he felt such an immediate and over-riding attraction to another human being.

'We've met before,' she said.

He nodded. 'A long time ago.'

She moved towards him and when he took her hands, she was trembling slightly. 'What are you thinking?'

'That I'd like to take you away now – this minute – to some quiet place where no one could touch us.'

'Is there such a place?'

'Only in dreams.'

She laughed shakily, pulled her hands free and took a cigarette from the box on the table. He gave her a light and she smiled.

'I think you must have been about nine years old when I first fell in love with you.'

'Is that a fact now?'

'Oh, yes.' She nodded seriously. 'I used to hang around your mother's shop on the off-chance that you might come out.'

'I always thought you hated me.'

'Not you – Bella. Everything male in the district from the kids upwards thought she was the last word. I never minded till you joined in.'

'It would seem I've got quite a lot to make up for,' he said calmly and when she turned to look up at him steadily, her eyes were sea-green, so deep a man could drown in them.

She took a deep breath, as if pulling herself back sharply to reality. 'Bella said you wanted a word with me about Ben.'

'That's right. She didn't seem very pleased about you coming to see us.'

'Bella's been putting off what she should do today till tomorrow, ever since I've been old enough to understand her,' Jean Fleming said. 'If it was left to her, she'd pretend Ben didn't exist and never had. That's no good. No good at all.'

'I've done a little checking with some of his old friends,' Nick said. 'He's definitely in town.'

Her head came up sharply. 'You've no idea where he is now?'

'None at all. I thought he might come here.'

'Oh, God. I hope not.'

She walked away from him, obviously in deep distress, and Nick frowned. 'What can he do? Kick up a fuss, be a little unpleasant, that's all. Anything more and we run him in.'

'That's what Harry said.'

She reached out momentarily, almost as if she would recover the words and Nick said: 'So you told him about the letter?'

She nodded. 'Bella didn't want to, so I went to him behind her back. She still isn't aware that Harry knows. That's why I wasn't completely honest with Superintendent Grant. I thought that if Ben turned up in town and the police had a word with him, that would be enough.'

'What did Faulkner say when you told him?'

'He laughed about it. Said he could have Ben taken care of any time he wanted. He also said I was more worried about myself than Bella in this business.'

'And are you?'

'I suppose I am if I am honest. If Ben turned up here now, created a scene and had to be arrested, the scandal would brush off Bella within a week at the most. It could ruin me.'

'The school, you mean?'

She nodded. 'I can just see the newspaper reports. A headmistress with a brother-in-law released from prison after a ten-year sentence for armed robbery. They'd have a field day.'

'It means a lot to you, doesn't it?'

'Oakdene?' She laughed. 'It isn't even mine. Not completely, anyway. When Miss Van Heflin had to retire unexpectedly and offered to sell me the school, I didn't have the necessary capital.'

'Wouldn't Faulkner help?'

A muscle tightened in her right cheek. 'That kind of assistance, I don't need. Not from him. Miss Van Heflin suggested I should pay her a percentage of the annual profit for an agreed period.'

'And it's worked out all right?'

'Another five years and it's all mine.'

There was real pride in her face and he grinned. 'A long way from Khyber Street.'

'That's what Superintendent Grant said.' She smiled. 'A long way for both of us.'

He took her hands and held them tightly. 'I'd like to see more of you, Jean. A lot more.'

She moved into his arms and touched him gently

on the face. 'I don't think you could get rid of me if you wanted to, now.'

They stayed there for a moment and then she pulled gently away. 'I'd like to have a few words with Bella, then you could take me home. I didn't bring my car. Or are you staying?'

He shook his head. 'I don't think so. I'd like to see Chuck Lazer before I go, though. Do you know him?'

'He used to play at Ben's club in the old days. He's the best there is. I'll look for you in there after I've seen Bella.'

She turned to the door and he caught her hand. 'I wouldn't like to be responsible for what might happen if I do see you home.'

Her face was very calm, the eyes fathomless. 'Then I'll be responsible.'

The door closed behind her softly. For a long time, he stood looking after her and then he started to move. Life could certainly be complicated and that was the understatement of the evening for a start.

When he went into the Long Room, Chuck Lazer was really high, way out on the edge of a cloud in a cool and quiet place where no one could touch him. After a while, he came back to earth slowly, his fingers crawling down the keyboard in a series of intricate chords and opened his eyes.

No one was listening and half the couples on the floor kept on dancing as though the music was still playing. As Lazer recognized him, Nick grinned sympathetically.

'You were on your own, man. Nobody heard.'

'Depends on your point of view, General. They were all out there with me, alive or dead, makes no difference. Fats and Bix, Jack Teagarden, Charlie Parker, Goodman, Billie Holliday. Anyone there ever was or ever will be.'

Nick offered him a cigarette, gave him a light. 'How about a drink?'

The American shook his head, ran the back of a hand across his forehead to wipe away the sweat. 'I need more than any drink, General, for what ails me.'

'I was speaking to your doctor earlier tonight,' Nick said carefully. 'He seems to think there's some hope for you.'

'Don't they always?'

'A new treatment,' Nick said. 'Not really new, but it's been tried successfully.'

'What's it involve. Withdrawal?'

'With the assistance of a drug called apomorphine. Prevents withdrawal symptoms and cuts out the craving for the usual stuff.'

'Sounds too good to be true.'

'How did you get hooked in the first place?'

Lazer shrugged. 'The wrong kind of party, too

much booze. Someone gave me a shot for a giggle after I passed out. That's all it took.'

Nick's hand balled up into a fist on top of the piano, the knuckles gleaming whitely, and Lazer grinned. 'I know, General, that's just how I felt.' He got to his feet abruptly. 'Sit in for me a couple of minutes, will you? I need a fix.'

He pushed his way through the crowd to a door in the corner by the bar. Nick sat down, nodded to the bass man and drummer and moved straight into a solid, pushing arrangement of 'St Louis Blues.' He was into the third chorus when Lazer returned. Nick started to slow, but the American shook his head, sat on the edge of the stool beside him and joined in.

The volume increased gradually with the tempo, Lazer gauging the length of each break expertly, Nick responding in the bass. Quite suddenly, there was something there, something different that had the couples on the floor turning in surprise to move towards the piano, crowding in, drawn by something that was real, that was as elemental as life itself.

Without changing the tempo, Lazer moved into 'How High the Moon' and Nick, challenged by the brilliant phrasing, countered with a rhythm pattern that had the American crying out in delight, head thrown back.

His hands found a richer theme and Nick

balanced with an intricate series of chords, dissolving into an eight-bar break that left his arms aching. He started to slow and Lazer followed him, down to the valley after the mountaintop, the quiet places where they finally faded in a minor key.

People were applauding all around and Lazer grinned, his eyes shining feverishly. 'You've been there, General. You've been there.'

Jean pushed through the crowd, her face glowing with surprise, and reached out to take his hand as he got to his feet. 'One of my minor vices,' Nick said with a grin. 'Are you ready to go?'

There was a slight tap on his shoulder and he turned to find Craig standing there, a polite, remote smile on the craggy face.

'Mr Faulkner's compliments, sir. If you'd be kind enough to follow me, I'll take you to him. He'd like a few words before you leave.'

15

Although Nick had never met Harry Faulkner personally, he had seen him at a distance on many occasions and knew that his brother met him now and then at clubs of the sort frequented by the wealthier business men of the town.

Respectable business man with wide interests, philanthropist, sportsman, chairman of several charities. That was the image he liked to cultivate. Harry Faulkner had come a long way from the riverside slum where he'd first seen the light of day and he wore his possessions for all to see, like the fresh gardenia in his buttonhole daily, his house in St Martin's Wood, his cars, his beautiful young wife.

And he had won all these things, his position in society, by breaking the law or, at least, by using it for his own ends. All his life he had worked on the fringe of the underworld, using his brains to make others do the things he wouldn't do himself, always careful so that whatever happened, whatever went wrong, nothing could touch Harry Faulkner.

He was sitting at the desk in his study when Nick was shown in, a stockily built man of middle height who carried his sixty years lightly. Even the iron grey hair somehow gave an impression of force and vitality.

Craig withdrew and Faulkner got to his feet and came round the desk, hand outstretched, a pleasant smile on his face. 'So you're Nick. I've heard a lot about you. Play golf at the club with your brother regularly.'

'Is that so?' Nick said.

'How about a drink? Whisky all right?'

'Irish if you have it.'

He sat on the edge of the desk as Faulkner went behind the bar. He was wearing one of the most beautiful dinner jackets Nick had ever seen, superbly cut and somehow right up to date without being too far out. His pleated shirt front gleamed in the fire-light, the cuff-links had just the right touch of ostenation.

There wasn't a hair out of place as he busied himself with the drinks, looking like something in an advertisement for good whisky in one of the better magazines. He was too perfect. It was as if someone had given him a list containing all the characteristics of a gentleman and he had ticked them off one by one.

He handed Nick one of the glasses and sat down behind the desk again. The whiskey was Jameson's and Nick savoured the inimitable flavour with conscious pleasure.

'Excellent,' he said.

'Glad you like it.' Faulkner carefully fitted a cigarette into a silver holder and leaned back in his chair. 'I've just had a little chat with Bella about this whole business. It's a pity that damned sister-in-law of mine can't keep her nose out of other people's affairs.'

'She seems to think it *is* her affair.'

'She would,' Faulkner said. 'All she can think of is that precious school of hers.'

'So you're not worried about Ben Garvald turning up here and causing any trouble?'

'He wouldn't be such a mug,' Faulkner said crisply, his accent slipping a little. 'I can look after my own. If Garvald doesn't know that by now, then it's time he learned.'

'An interesting point.' Nick swallowed a little more of his Jameson's. 'Someone tried to teach Ben a lesson outside Wandsworth when he was released yesterday morning. From what I hear, they came badly unstuck.'

'These things happen all the time,' Faulkner said blandly. 'All you need's a little bit of fog and every

147

tearaway in town turns out to see what he can pick up.'

'Strange you should say that,' Nick said. 'Although we didn't have any fog up here, it was quite thick around Wandsworth yesterday morning.'

Faulkner had stopped smiling. 'What's that supposed to mean?'

'It means that a lump of dung called Sammy Rosco arranged the hit outside Wandsworth. He made a mistake. So did Fred Manton.'

Faulkner's face was quite expressionless. 'And what's Manton got to do with this?'

'That's the interesting part. From what I can make out, he was acting as middleman for a friend. Now I wonder who that could be?'

When Faulkner answered, his accent had slipped right back to the canal docks and his eyes sparkled viciously. 'If you've got anything to say, spit it out and be sure you can make it stick because I'll take you all the way.'

Nick swallowed the rest of his Jameson's, walked to the bar and helped himself to another. 'All right, it goes something like this. When Bella got that note from Ben the other day, she didn't want to tell you because she's the kind who thinks that if you close your eyes to a situation and pretend it's not there, maybe it'll go away. But her sister's built differently. She decided, on balance, that it would be better if you were told.'

'So?'

'You had a word with Manton, told him to arrange a reception for Ben when he got out of Wandsworth. The only kind of reception you thought he'd understand.' Nick grinned. 'You made a bad error there.'

'Finished?' Faulkner asked.

'I wonder what he wants with Bella?' Nick said. 'Maybe he'd like her back. She might even go with him. From what I hear, they used to be pretty thick in the old days.'

Faulkner's anger overflowed like hot lava and he jabbed viciously at a button on the desk. 'Who in the hell do you think you're talking to?'

'Big Harry Faulkner, the punter's friend,' Nick said. 'Business man philanthropist, a dream at the orphans' Christmas party every year. Also thief, whoremaster and pimp.' He emptied his glass and put it down on top of the bar. 'Tell me something, Faulkner. I know those Gascoigne Street brothels of yours can supply any kind of female anyone ever wanted, but is it true you run a special line in the male variety as well?'

The door opened and Craig entered. He moved to the desk and Faulkner, his face ashen, raised a trembling hand. 'Throw him out.'

Craig turned slowly to face Nick, his fingers opening and closing. 'You know, I didn't like the look of you from the moment you walked in.'

He seemed very sure of himself. When he was about three feet away, he swung a tremendous punch that carried everything he had.

Nick moved in close, catching the blow with a karate block delivered with his left hand and kicked the big man viciously on the shin, lifting his right knee into the unprotected face as Craig doubled over.

He lay on his back moaning, a hand to his mouth, blood trickling between his fingers. 'Get up, Craig! Get up!' Faulkner ordered.

'I don't think he's going to be quite that stupid.' Nick walked across to the door. He turned with it half open, the dark eyes sending a cold shiver through Faulkner. 'There's more to this than shows on the surface, Faulkner. Much more. I'll be back when I find out what it is.'

Jean was standing at the entrance to the Long Room, a light evening coat over one arm, a jewelled bag swinging from the other. 'What did Harry want?'

'Nothing special. Ready to go?'

Before she could answer, Chuck Lazer pushed through the crowd. 'Leaving, General?'

Nick nodded. 'It's been sweet, but we've got to go.'

'Mind if I string along? I've had enough of this wake.'

Nick turned to Jean with a grin. 'A chaperon. That just about settles everything.'

'I wouldn't be too sure,' she said as he held her coat for her and, when they moved towards the door, they were laughing.

Faulkner moved round the desk and kicked Craig in the side. 'Go on, get out!'

Craig scrambled away from him, dodging another blow, got to his feet and wrenched open the door. As it closed behind him, Faulkner went to the bar and poured himself another whisky. He emptied the glass in two swallows, coughing as the liquor burned its way into his stomach.

For some strange reason, Miller reminded him of his teacher at Dock Road Elementary, old Walter Street who'd had a hard war in the trenches in the first lot and walked with a limp.

He remembered the first time he'd met Street after leaving school. He was nineteen, already living on the earnings of three women, dressed up to the nines in the best money could buy. He'd been a mug, really, trying to come the big man and old Walter in his shabby trenchcoat had looked at him as if he were a lump of dung he'd be glad to scrape off his shoe.

He hurled the glass into the fireplace, moved across to the bedroom and opened the door. Bella was standing in front of the mirror by the bed, pulling the red dress over her head. The flame coloured slip she was wearing had lifted over her rounded haunches and white flesh gleamed at the top of a dark stocking.

'What are you doing?' he demanded hoarsely.

'Ringing the changes. I'm wearing the black one next. Give me a hand, will you? This damned zip has broken.'

He stood beside her, reaching to pull the dress over her head, conscious of the warmth, the sweetness. He slid his hands under the armpits, cupping the full breasts, pulling her hard against him.

'For God's sake, Harry,' she said impatiently. 'There are a hundred and twenty people out there.'

As she turned, all the rage, all the anger and frustration boiled over and he slapped her across the face. 'Don't tell me what to do!' he shouted. 'I'm Harry Faulkner, understand? And you're my wife and you'll do whatever I say!'

She started to back away, fear on her face, and the sight of it made the blood race through his veins like fire. He grabbed for the neck of the slip, ripping it from top to bottom and she staggered, falling back across the bed.

He flung himself on her, hands sliding across her breasts, mouth reached for hers and as always, she responded, running her fingers through his hair, kissing him passionately.

And it was no good. It was just like all the other times. The strength, the emotion, drained out of him and he pushed himself up and looked down at her, a dazed expression in his eyes. When he turned to the mirror, an old man stared out at him.

'Can I get dressed now?' she said calmly.

He walked to the door like a dead man, opened it and turned, moistening dry lips. 'I'm sorry, Bella. I don't know what got into me.'

'That's all right, Harry.'

She stood looking at him, magnificent, the torn slip hanging around her waist, but there was only pity in her eyes and that was not what he wanted. He closed the door, went to his desk and pressed the buzzer. There was still a power he could command, a certain kind of power. That was better than nothing.

After a while, the door opened and Craig came in, his lips bruised and swelling. 'Yes, Mr Faulkner?'

'Has Miller left?'

'About five minutes ago. It looked to me as if he was taking your sister-in-law home.'

'Just her type.' Faulkner ground his cigarette viciously into the ashtray. 'It's time he was cut down to size, Craig – and I mean cut. Are you with me?'

'Perfectly,' Craig said, his face wooden. 'I'll see to it, Mr Faulkner.'

'I wouldn't waste any time if I were you. He mightn't be at the schoolhouse long.'

'Fifteen minutes is all it takes, Mr Faulkner.'

Craig withdrew and Faulkner went to the bar and poured himself a large tonic water. He drank it slowly, savouring the freshness, and after a while the bedroom door opened and Bella appeared.

She looked quite beautiful, her face freshly made up, a three-quarter length dress of black lace moulding her magnificent body.

'Ready, Harry?' she said brightly.

He took both her hands and shook his head. 'My God, but I'm proud of you, Bella. You're the most beautiful damned thing in there tonight.'

She kissed his cheek affectionately and took his arm. When they opened the door to return to the party, they were smiling.

16

The flat overlooked the school yard and when Nick drew the curtain and peered into the night, rain hammered relentlessly into the asphalt and fog crowded the spiked railings, yellow in the glow of the street lamps.

'How many kids have you got?' he called.

Jean Fleming answered from the bedroom. 'One hundred and fifty-three. I could double it with no trouble, but you can't get the staff these days.'

As he turned, he caught a glimpse of her through the half open door beside the bed, her supple body outlined boldly under the nylon slip as she unfastened her stockings.

He watched as she continued to undress, curiously detached about the whole thing, not even conscious of the overwhelming physical attraction he had experienced earlier.

The secret graces of a woman's body. Something

utterly fundamental to life itself, something of the quiet places where a man could find peace. *Was this what he wanted?*

He turned and looked down into the rain again, and from the music room below the sound of Chuck Lazer's playing rose into the night. He was working his way through all the standards, Berlin, Cole Porter, Rogers and Hart. The kind of stuff nobody seemed to be writing any more. A hint of summer that had gone and memories only now.

Jean came into the room wearing a pair of dark trews and a quilted jacket, her face wiped clean of make-up so that she seemed startlingly young and innocent.

'What would you like – coffee or tea?'

'Tea if that's all right with you, then I must be going.'

Her smile was replaced by a slight frown. 'Must you?'

He nodded. 'I'm still on duty.'

She went into the kitchen and filled the kettle and he leaned in the doorway watching her. She prepared a tray, spooned tea into an old brown pot, then sat on a stool, hugging her knees, waiting for the kettle to boil.

They had lost something, some essential contact they had found earlier, and Nick searched quickly for the right note.

'It's much larger than I expected.'

'The school?' She nodded. 'At first there was just this old house and then Miss Van Heflin had extensions made. We have additional classrooms at the rear now. You can only see them properly in daylight.'

'How long have you been here?'

'Five years. Ever since I qualified. When Ben was arrested, I didn't think I'd be able to continue my training. The Principal of the teaching college where I was supposed to be going wrote to say he couldn't offer me a place after all.'

'What did you do?'

'At first I cried, then I got mad.' She smiled. 'Funny how a kick in the teeth brings out the best in you. Somehow a teaching college wasn't good enough after that so I decided to go to University. Bella couldn't help. She had enough on her plate, but I managed to get a small grant from the local authority. I made it up by working in the vacations. One year I even took a job as a barmaid in the evenings.'

'That must have been tough.'

'It wasn't as bad as it sounds. When I got my degree, I came here to work for Miss Van Heflin. She was marvellous.'

'Things always seem to come out right in the end if you live right.'

As the kettle boiled, she moved to the stove and started to fill the teapot. 'What about you?'

'Nothing as complicated. Phil was keen on me going to University and the way the business expanded, I certainly never had to worry about money. I went to the London School of Economics and read law.'

'And then found you didn't want to become a lawyer?'

'Something like that.'

'But why the police?'

'Why not?'

'You know what I mean.'

'Perfectly. I get it from Phil at least twice a day. Labourers in uniform, a working man's profession. Big men, small brains. Isn't that how it runs?'

'I didn't say that.'

'No one ever does, but that's roughly what they mean.'

He was suddenly angry. He walked back into the other room, opened the window and leaned into the rain. She followed him in, placed the tray on the table and moved to his side.

'I'm sorry, Nick. Truly I am.'

He grinned tightly. 'People are funny. A solicitor misappropriates a client's funds, a schoolmaster criminally assaults a child; they get what they deserve. No more, no less. But no one would dream of attacking either of their professions as a whole. That kind of reasoning never applies where the police are concerned.'

'I said I was sorry.'

'When the chips are down, people always are. When they need help, they can't reach a telephone fast enough.'

She placed a hand on his sleeve and when she spoke, her voice was strangely subdued. 'It means a lot to you, doesn't it?'

He looked down at her, no expression in those strange dark eyes, but there was a harsh finality in his voice. 'I wouldn't be anything else. Not now or ever, Jean.'

And then she smiled and her hand reached up to touch his face in a gesture that meant more than any kiss. 'That's all right then, isn't it? Come and have your tea.'

They sat by the fire in companionable silence and Nick drank his tea and watched her. She closed her eyes and rested her head against the back of the chair looking strangely defenceless.

'Tell me something,' he said. 'About Ben – are you worried? Really worried, I mean?'

She opened her eyes and it was there, no need for her to try to put it into words. 'All my life I wanted to get out of Khyber Street. And I managed it, Nick. I'm where I want to be in a calmer, more ordered world. And now Ben has to come back to spoil it all.' The knuckles of her hands gleamed whitely as her fingers interlaced. 'God, how I hate him.'

Nick leaned forward, a slight frown on his face. 'You really mean that, don't you?'

'I've always hated him.' She got to her feet and walked to the window. 'I was fourteen when he married Bella and from the day she brought him back to live with us, my life became a sort of nightmare.' She turned suddenly. 'No, that isn't quite true. It's just that whenever I turned, he seemed to be there watching me. When I was dressing or undressing. I'd find him in the doorway, that smile on his face.'

She shuddered visibly and Nick's throat went dry. 'Go on.'

'There isn't anything else. Not what you mean, anyway. He was too clever for that. But there were other things.' She stared into the past. 'He was so damned strong. When he put those great hands of his on me there was nothing I could do – nothing.'

'Didn't you ever try speaking to Bella?'

'I threatened to do just that, but he only laughed. Said she wouldn't have believed a word and he was right.'

Nick got to his feet and took her in his arms gently. When he pulled her close, she started to tremble. 'That was a long time ago. Long gone. Ben Garvald will never trouble you again, I promise you that.'

She stared up into his face and then her hands

slid around his neck, pulling down his head, her mouth opening beneath his. As the blood surged in his temples, Nick slid his hands over her buttocks, holding her fiercely against him.

Through the turbulence he was aware that she was repeating his name over and over again and he closed his eyes and hung on, waiting for the roaring to diminish. After a while, he opened them again and smiled down at her.

'I wonder what the Sunday supplements would make of this? I can see the headlines now. Case of the Amorous Detective.'

She smiled up at him, her eyes bright. 'To hell with the Sunday supplements.'

'I know,' he said. 'But I've still got to go.'

She sighed deeply and pushed herself away from him. 'Any chance of your coming back?'

'I'm afraid not. I'll give you a ring tomorrow. Maybe we could have dinner.'

'I'd better give you my number.'

'Isn't it in the book?'

'Only the school office, not the flat.' She smiled. 'A trick of the trade. If it was, I'd have half a dozen parents phoning through every evening. I'd never know a moment's peace.'

She rummaged in a drawer, found a folded piece of notepaper, and quickly scribbled her name and telephone number on it. She folded it again, slipped it into his inside pocket and smiled up at him.

'No excuses now.'

'None at all.'

'Especially if you have this.' She took a Yale key on a ring from her pocket and held it up. 'If you *can* get back before breakfast, let yourself in.'

'Won't you be in bed?'

'I should imagine so.'

She smiled delightfully and he pulled her close and kissed her again. 'Now let's get out of here before I'm completely corrupted.'

Chuck was still sitting at the upright piano in the corner of the music room playing by the light of the street lamp that drifted in through the window.

'End of score,' Nick called softly from the doorway.

Chuck ended on a fast run of intricate chords, swung round and stood up. 'I'm with you, General. Where to now?'

'I want to check in at Headquarters,' Nick said. 'I can drop you off at your place if you like.'

They moved into the small porch a few yards from the side gate in the railings. The rain still hammered down through the fog and Jean shivered.

'Rather you than me.'

He grinned down at her. 'Pity the poor copper. I'll see you.'

They walked across the yard, opened the side

gate and moved along the narrow pavement. The street was little more than an alley and bordered on the other side by a high stone wall.

The Mini-Cooper was parked under an old-fashioned gas lamp and Nick took the keys from his pocket as he stepped off the pavement to reach the off-side. From the lighted porch, Jean called his name urgently.

As he started to turn, a fist lifted into his face and some inexplicable reflex caused him to duck so that the blow glanced from his cheek. He was aware of sharp pain as a metal ring sliced his skin like a razor and then his hand swung expertly as he turned, catching his assailant across the side of the neck.

The man staggered back towards the outer darkness beyond the light thrown out by the gas lamp and Nick was aware of others. Three, perhaps four, he couldn't be sure because they came out of the fog with a sudden rush like a rugby forward line.

One of them held an iron bar in both hands. As he came within striking distance it swung up and down, the man grunting with the effort. Nick ducked and the bar thudded across the roof of the car. He lifted his foot savagely into the man's crutch, the bar rang against the cobbles and the man collapsed with a choking cry.

There was no time for words. Two more came boring in, one of them wielding a bone-handled razor, the blade gleaming dully in the rain. Nick reached for the wrist, turning his head to avoid a blow from the other and was aware of Jean Fleming's face beyond the man's shoulder, contorted with anger, teeth bared.

She hooked her fingers into long, greasy hair, dragging the man's head back and Nick concentrated on the other. He swung in, pushing the razor away from him and applied a wrist lock. The man screamed, dropping the razor, and Nick delivered an elbow strike at close quarters that produced a cry of agony.

The man fell backwards, got to his feet and stumbled away. Nick turned and found Lazer rolling in the flooded gutter, grappling with a man in an old trenchcoat. Jean was against the wall, struggling furiously.

Nick moved in fast, grabbed the man by the collar with both hands and sent him staggering into the fog. At the same moment, Lazer's assailant rolled on top, got to his feet and went after his comrades fast.

There was silence. Only the rain hissing down, Jean struggling to catch her breath, a slight moan from the one who had carried the iron bar.

Lazer, sitting in the gutter, got to his feet with a queer, choking laugh. 'What brought that little lot on?'

'I think I must have hurt somebody's feelings.' Nick turned to Jean. 'You all right?'

She laughed shakily. 'You're damned right I am. What on earth was it all about?'

'I don't know, Jean.' He shook his head. 'There's more to this whole business than meets the eye. Much more.'

There was a slight noise behind them and as he swung round, the man who was lying face down on the pavement beside the car, reached for the iron bar and started to his feet. Lazer moved across quickly, pulled it easily from his grasp and slammed the man hard against the car.

'Another move like that and I'll bend this across your skull.'

The man hung there, hands clawing across the roof for support, head down and Nick took Jean by the arm and led her to the gate. 'Mix yourself a stiff drink, you've earned it. Then go to bed.'

She looked up at him anxiously, her face pale in the lamplight. 'What about you?'

'I'll take this character down to Central with me, not that I expect to get very much out of him. On the other hand we should be able to put him away for a couple of years, which is something.'

'Can you get back later on?'

'I'll try, I really will.' He took her hand and held it tightly for a moment. 'You looked good in there.'

'The Khyber Street brand goes clear to the bone,' she said. 'You can never quite get rid of it.' She took a handkerchief from her pocket and reached up to dab the blood on his right cheek. 'That's a nasty cut. It needs looking at.'

He caught her wrist gently, pulled her close in his arms and kissed her and it was like nothing he had ever experienced before, touching something deep inside him, fierce yet gentle.

She stared up at him, an expression of wonder in her eyes, and then she smiled and it was as if a lamp had been turned on inside. She reached up and touched his face once, then ran through the rain across the yard to the porch.

17

The pale green walls of the Interrogation Room seemed to swim out of the shadows caused by the strong central light hanging above the table at which sat Charles Edward Foster, head in hands, his entire body one great ache.

Nick stood at the window and looked into the deserted rainswept street outside. His cheek throbbed painfully and he gingerly prodded the broad strip of sticking plaster with a finger end.

It was a little after two-fifteen. He yawned, took out a crumpled packet of cigarettes and extracted the last one. He was in the act of lighting it when the Duty Inspector entered.

'I've filled in the charge sheet for you.'

'I'll remember you in my will.'

'I think your next move should be to the Infirmary. That's a nasty cut you've got there. Probably needs a stitch or two.'

Foster raised his head. 'Never mind that bastard. What about me? I need a doctor if anyone does after what he did. Just wait till my solicitor gets here.'

'And just what did he do to you, Charlie?' Superintendent Grant said from the doorway.

Foster contrived an expression that was a mixture of innocent mystification and hurt dignity. 'Kicked me in the crutch, he did, Mr Grant. You've got a right one here, I can tell you.'

The Inspector handed the charge sheet to Grant without a word.

'Presumably this little lot has got nothing to do with the case at all?'

Grant walked across to a side table on which were laid neatly the iron bar, bone-handled razor and length of bicycle chain which had been left on the scene of battle by Foster's friends.

Foster lapsed into sullen silence and Grant looked enquiringly at Nick. 'All right, are you?'

'He needs a few stitches in that face, if you ask me, sir,' the Duty Inspector put in.

Grant nodded. 'Have somebody take this cowboy downstairs will you, Jack? I'll have a word with him later.'

The Inspector nodded, took Foster by the arm and led him out. Grant sat on the edge of the table and lit his pipe.

'You've heard about Brady?'

'When I brought Foster in. What happened exactly?'

'Looks like a hit and run. We had an anonymous 999 call, but that doesn't mean anything. Probably some good citizen who didn't want to dirty his hands by getting mixed up in police business.' He sighed. 'What a night. A factory break-in at Maske Lane that'll push the crime figures up by £7,000 at least. God knows how many smash and grabs in the log, three robberies with assault, obviously the same artist, and one attempted rape. On top of that, this Brady business.'

'How is he?'

'There's the preliminary report if you're interested.'

'It doesn't look too good, does it?' Nick said, handing the casualty report back to Grant.

'They turned out a Consultant and I had a word with him after his examination. Apparently the skull fracture's the only really serious part. The rest is just trimmings. As things are at the moment, he doesn't see why Jack shouldn't pull through.' He sighed and applied another match to his pipe. 'I'd like to know what he was doing in Canal Street, though.'

Nick crushed his cigarette into the ashtray. 'Did you know that after leaving here, he went looking for Ben Garvald?'

Grant stared at him blankly, a look of genuine

amazement on his face. 'What in the hell are you talking about? Ben Garvald is your pigeon.'

'Which didn't stop Brady visiting the Flamingo before me to ask Fred Manton if Garvald had been around.'

'You're sure about this?'

'Manton told me himself.' Nick shrugged. 'I can't see any reason for him to lie.'

Grant frowned heavily, his teeth clamped hard on the stem of his pipe. 'I wonder what Jack was playing at?'

'I think it's simple enough,' Nick said. 'He finds me pretty hard to take. Perhaps he thought he'd be proving something if he got to Garvald first.'

Grant sighed heavily. 'You could be right. In any case, we won't know anything for sure until he regains consciousness.'

'What about the car that hit him?'

'A needle in a haystack on a night like this, but we'll find it, never fear.' Grant applied yet another match to the bowl of his pipe. 'You'd better fill me in on what you've been up to. You've certainly stamped good and hard on somebody's toes when they go to the expense of putting Charlie Foster and his gallant band on to you.'

Nick filled in the details quickly, leaving nothing out. When he was finished, Grant sat there, a frown on his weatherbeaten face.

'What do you think?' Nick asked after a while.

'I think it stinks,' Grant said, 'to high heaven. When you get cautious birds like Fred Manton and Harry Faulkner allowing themselves to be dragged down, there must be a reason.' He stood up abruptly. 'Find Ben Garvald, Miller. He's the key.'

Nick picked up his cap and coat from a chair and grinned tightly. 'It's a great life if you don't weaken.'

'Not at half past bloody two in the morning with the sodding Asian flu seeping into your bones it isn't,' Grant said. 'I'll have Aspro coming out of my ears if I take any more. Keep in touch. I'll be at that factory in Maske Lane if you need me.'

He walked away along the corridor to his office and Nick pulled on his coat and cap and went downstairs to the main entrance. Chuck Lazer leaned in a corner, eyes closed.

Nick nodded to the desk sergeant and touched Lazer on the shoulder. 'Let's go, America.'

He moved out through the glass doors and paused at the top of the main steps beside a tall pillar, pulling up his collar against the rain.

'What happens now?' Lazer demanded as he joined him.

Nick grinned. 'For you, bed. I'll drop you off at your place. I'm still on duty till six and a lot later than that if I don't find Garvald.'

'It's that important, is it?'

Chuck Lazer hesitated. 'Look, you meant what you said earlier, didn't you? About only wanting a chat with Ben? I mean, he hasn't done anything, has he?'

'Not that I know of, but he could certainly clear a few things up for us,' Nick frowned. 'Don't tell me you know where he is?'

Lazer made his decision and sighed. 'He said something about the Regent Hotel, General. It's not far from City Square. That doesn't mean he'll be in, mind you.'

'Maybe not, but it's something to go on,' Nick said and together they hurried down the steps to the Mini-Cooper.

When they went into the foyer of the Regent Hotel, it was deserted. Nick rang the bell and after a while, the door to the office opened and the Irish girl came out, sleep in her eyes. She straightened the skirt of her nylon overall and yawned.

'What can I do for you?'

'Police,' Nick said. 'I'm looking for a man called Garvald – Ben Garvald. I understand he's staying here. Probably booked in this evening.'

Something moved in her eyes, but it was quickly gone and she managed a puzzled frown. 'There's been some mistake. We don't have any Mr Garvald staying here.'

172

'He could be using another name. A big, toughlooking Irishman. Aged about forty.'

'No. We've nobody like that.' She shook her head positively. 'As a matter of fact, we've only had two new guests in the last three days and they were a couple of Indian gentlemen.'

'Can I see the register?'

She produced it from beneath the counter without a flicker and he opened it. The last signatures halfway down a page were two days old – the Indians she had mentioned. If the book was any guide, she was certainly telling the truth.

'Satisfied, Sergeant?' she said brightly.

Nick smiled and closed the register. 'Sorry you've been troubled. Must be some other hotel.'

Lazer had said nothing throughout the interview, but when they got outside into the street, he grabbed Nick by the sleeve. 'The Regent Hotel, Gloyne Street. That's what the man said, General.'

'I know, I know,' Nick said. 'She's lying. It stuck out a mile. Give it a couple of minutes and we'll go back in.'

He lit a cigarette and stood there on the bottom step just inside the porch, staring into the rain, feeling suddenly tired. He hadn't got his second wind yet, that was the trouble. He flicked the cigarette through the darkness in a gleaming curve, nodded to Lazer and pushed the glass door open softly.

The foyer was deserted again, but the office door stood ajar. He moved forward quietly and gently raised the flap of the reception desk.

The Irish girl was standing at the office desk, a handbag open in front of her. She took a wad of notes from it quickly, put one foot on a chair, slid back her skirt and pushed the notes into her stocking top.

Lazer clapped his hands together gently. 'Now that's what I really call a show.'

The Irish girl swung round, straightening her skirt, alarm on her face. For a moment, she seemed shaken and uncertain and then obviously decided to brazen it out.

'Hey, is that nice, sneaking up on a girl like that?'

'Oh, we didn't think you'd mind.' Nick took her hands. 'What's your name, sweetheart?'

'Aren't you the one?' As he pushed her back against the desk, she put her arms around his neck. 'And what would the Chief Constable say to this, I wonder?'

'He likes us to have our fun. After all, that's what keeps us going.'

He leaned down to kiss her and at the same moment, slid his right hand quickly up a warm leg. She started to struggle, but he found what he was looking for and grinned as he held up the wad of notes.

'Give me that, damn you,' she said, striking out at him, trying to grab his hand. 'What in the hell do you think you're playing at?'

He shoved her away and counted the money quickly. 'Twenty quid and all in oncers.' He shook his head. 'You've never had this much together at any one time in your life before.'

'You give me my money,' she spat, tears of rage in her eyes.

He flung it in her face and as she staggered back with a cry, grabbed her by the shoulders and shook her viciously. 'Ten seconds, that's all I'm going to give you. Garvald was here, wasn't he?'

She cracked wide open, terror in her eyes, arms up before her face to block the blow she expected to follow. 'Don't hit me for God's sake. I'll tell you! I'll tell you!'

Nick stood back and waited and after a moment or two, the words came tumbling out. 'He came in this evening, about nine o'clock. He didn't sign the book because I forgot to ask him to.'

'Did he go out?'

'Not as far as I know. He was in at one o'clock when the men came for him.'

'Who were they?' She hesitated and he took a quick step towards her, his voice grating. 'I said who were they?'

'One of them was a bloke I met at a party a few weeks ago. A Greek or a Cypriot or something.

175

They called him Jango. I don't know who the other was. He had a wall eye, that's all I can tell you.'

'Max Donner,' Lazer put in quickly. 'He and Jango are a couple of heavies. Manton keeps them around to handle the rough stuff.'

Nick nodded and turned back to the girl. 'So they gave you twenty quid. What for?'

'I had to take Mr Garvald a cup of tea. Jango put something in it. Knock-out drops I suppose. I think they were afraid of him.'

'And it worked?'

She nodded. 'They took him away in a car. I don't know where to.'

Nick turned to Lazer and the American shrugged. 'Maybe the Flamingo?'

'I shouldn't think it's very likely,' Nick said. 'But we can try.'

They turned to the door and the Irish girl grabbed his sleeve. 'I didn't mean any harm. They said they were friends of his, that they were just playing a joke on him.'

'Do I look as if I came over on a banana boat?' Nick tapped her gently on the side of the face with his open hand. 'You've got twenty quid and there's a boat train leaving for Liverpool around 6 a.m. Be on it.'

He turned and walked out leaving her standing in the middle of the room. She stood there gazing at the open doorway for a while, a dazed expression on her face, then got down on her hands and knees wearily and started to pick up the money.

There was plenty of activity outside the Flamingo, mainly cars driving away, and Nick stood in a doorway opposite the Mini-Cooper and smoked a cigarette as he waited for Chuck Lazer.

The plot was thickening with a vengeance, so much was evident, but the reasons were still far from clear. One thing was certain. Whoever wanted Ben Garvald out of the way, must have a pretty good reason.

The American came round the corner from the alley and joined him in the doorway. 'No sign of them. Manton isn't there either.'

'You're sure?'

'Absolutely. I even went upstairs and searched his private apartment. Let myself out of the side door.' He shrugged. 'Maybe he's in the river already – Ben, I mean.'

'Is there anywhere else they could take him? Somewhere secluded or out of the way, perhaps.'

Lazer frowned and then suddenly his face lit up. 'Why didn't I think of it before? There's an old Georgian house on the edge of town near Ryescroft. They call it The Grange locally. Stands on its own in a couple of acres.'

'Is it Manton's?'

Lazer shook his head. 'Another of Faulkner's

buys. He's going to turn it into a swish country club, but Manton's in charge out there. At the moment, there's only a caretaker. Weird old boy called Bluey Squires. Used to be on the door at the Flamingo till he broke a leg.'

Ryescroft. That was half a mile beyond the city boundary which strictly speaking brought it within the jurisdiction of the county constabulary. Nick considered that along with several other important facts and made his decision.

'Let's get moving,' he said and went down the steps to the Mini-Cooper.

18

The Grange was the sort of place that had been built in grey Yorkshire stone on the high tide of Victorian prosperity by some self-made megalo-maniac. Vast Gothic chimneys lifted into the night from the pointed roof and the grounds were surrounded by a ten-foot wall.

Nick parked in a narrow lane some thirty or forty yards from the main gate, opened a door and got out. 'It looks like a bad set for *Wuthering Heights*.'

Lazer slid behind the wheel and grinned. 'Wish me luck, General. Maybe they'll give me a medal or something.'

'Play it by ear,' Nick told him. 'If Manton *is* there, you know what to say. I'll wait for you here.'

The American slammed the door and drove away rapidly. The iron gates stood open and he followed the drive between a double line of poplar trees leading up to the great dark pile of the house. No light showed anywhere and he took a narrower path that went round the side to a cobbled yard.

Light streamed from a rear window, falling across Manton's Jaguar, and Lazer switched off the engine. As the sound died into the night, a dog started to bark inside the house, hollow and menacing, touching something elemental inside him so that he shivered.

As he got out of the Mini-Cooper, the house door opened, a shaft of light picking him from the night.

'Who is it?' a hoarse voice croaked.

'It's Chuck Lazer, Bluey,' the American replied. 'I've been looking for Fred. Thought he might be here.'

Squires was sixty and looked older. Tousled grey hair fell across a broad forehead and he was badly in need of a shave. He carried a shotgun under his left arm and his right hand was clamped firmly around the collar of a magnificent black and silver Alsatian who strained eagerly towards Lazer, the growl rising from deep inside his throat like a volcano about to erupt.

'He's pretty busy,' Squires said. 'Is it important?'

'You're telling me it is,' Lazer moved forward. 'Are Donner and Jango here?'

The old man glared at him suspiciously. 'You want to know a hell of a lot, don't you?'

'What's all the mystery? I've been here before, haven't I?'

'All right, all right,' the old man said. 'I suppose you'd better come in.'

They entered what had obviously been the main kitchen of the house in its great days, a large, stone-flagged room with a black kitchen range and stove running along one side. It was dirty and untidy, the table in the centre cluttered with unwashed dishes, a couple of empty milk bottles, half a loaf of bread and several opened cans of food. The narrow bed in the corner was unmade.

Squires gave the Alsatian an order and it crouched in front of the fire, staring unwinkingly at the American. 'You wait here. I'll get Manton.'

He leaned the shotgun against the wall and went out. Lazer sat on the edge of the table. After a while, the door opened again and Manton entered, Donner behind him.

Manton had an overcoat hanging from his shoulders against the cold and he was frowning. 'I thought you were supposed to be playing at Faulkner's party?'

'I left,' Lazer said simply. 'Some lousy copper turned up asking about Ben Garvald. CID sergeant called Miller.'

'Ben Garvald?' Manton said. 'But he's still inside.'

'Not any more he isn't. They released him yesterday. According to this guy Miller, he's right here in town.'

'What do they want him for?'

'A routine enquiry, that's what the man said, but I figured you should know, Fred. You and Ben having been so close in the old days. Maybe this copper will be calling on you next.'

'You did right, Chuck. Thanks a lot.' Manton hesitated. 'This bloke Miller – did he mention my name?'

Lazer shook his head. 'He went off in one hell of a rush. Seems some detective or other was on the receiving end in a hit and run earlier tonight. He's in the Infirmary now hanging on by a thread.'

There was a stifled exclamation from Donner in the doorway and the skin seemed to stretch a little more tightly across Manton's face. He managed a ghastly smile.

'Sorting that little lot should keep them out of mischief till the morning. Thanks for the good word, Chuck. You did right to come.'

'That's all right then.' Lazer got to his feet. 'I'll be making tracks. It's time for some shut-eye.' He moved to the door, opened it and turned with a grin. 'See you at the club tomorrow.'

The door closed behind him and a small trapped

wind raced round the room, looking for a way out and died in a corner. It was Donner who broke the silence first.

'If Brady pulls through and talks . . .

'Fifteen years each,' Manton said in a whisper. 'There isn't a judge in the country would give less.'

'We could be in Liverpool by morning,' Donner said. 'A quick passage to Spain and no questions asked. I know the right people.'

'That kind of thing costs money.'

'Plenty in the safe at the club. Seven maybe eight grand.'

'Faulkner's, not mine.'

'We could go a long way.'

Manton made his decision and nodded. 'There's just one thing. What if the coppers are on to us already? They could be hanging around the club right now waiting for us to show.'

'That's an easy one.' Donner shrugged, his face quite calm. 'Send Jango. He'll find out for us.'

'But will he go?'

'I don't see why not.' Donner grinned. 'Especially if you don't tell him the score.'

Manton started to chuckle and shook his head. 'You're a hard bastard, Donner.'

'It's the only way,' Donner replied. 'What about Garvald?'

'No point in hanging on to him any longer. He should still be out cold. We'll take him with us and dump him on the side of the road going over the moors.'

Squires limped into the kitchen from the passage. 'Jango's gone to check on the bloke upstairs, Mr Manton. How long is he going to be with us?'

Before Manton could reply, there was a high-pitched cry from somewhere deep inside the house and he swung round quickly. 'That sounded like Jango!'

Without a word, Donner snatched up the shotgun and ran along the dark passage.

Ben Garvald drifted up from a wall of darkness and opened his eyes. The room was festooned with cobwebs – giant grey cobwebs that undulated slowly.

He closed his eyes and breathed deeply, fighting the panic which rose inside him. When he opened them again, the cobwebs had almost disappeared.

He was lying on a narrow bed against one wall of a small room. A shaded light hung down from the ceiling and curtains were drawn across the window.

He swung his legs to the floor and sat on the edge of the bed for a while before trying to stand. There was a bad taste in his mouth and his tongue was dry and swollen. Whatever had gone into that tea had been good – damned good.

He got to his feet and staggered across the room,

steadied himself against the wall, turned and moved back to the bed. After a while, the cobwebs disappeared completely and everything clicked back into place.

His room at the hotel, the Irish girl with her cup of tea, he remembered that. And then Donner had arrived, which could only mean one thing. The copper who'd gone down the stairs at the club had snuffed it.

An interesting situation. He got to his feet again and checked the door. It was securely fastened, a mortice deadlock from the look of things, and there was no transom. He crossed to the window and drew back the curtains. The sash lifted easily and he looked out.

He was on the top floor and the gardens lay forty feet below in the darkness. The nearest window was a good ten feet away to the left and impossible to reach.

He closed the window, moved back to the bed to consider the situation and a key rattled in the lock. For a moment he hesitated, then quickly got back on the bed and closed his eyes.

The door opened and someone walked across. Garvald waited and as a hand gripped his shirt front to shake him gently, opened his eyes and looked into the startled face of Jango. The Cypriot managed one cry of alarm before Garvald's right fist sank into his stomach. Jango keeled over, gasping for air, and Garvald got to his feet and moved out of the room quickly, closing the door behind him.

He descended a flight of stairs to the next landing and Donner's voice drifted up from the hall below. 'Jango! Jango, what's going on!'

Garvald opened the nearest door, stepped into the darkness of the room beyond and waited. There was a step on the bare floor-boards and Donner moved into view, the shotgun held at waist level. Garvald moved out into the corridor, the edge of his hand swinging down with numbing force against Donner's right arm. Donner grunted and dropped the shotgun.

'Watch it, Manton, Garvald's on the loose!' Donner called and threw himself at the big man, the fingers of his left hand hooking for the eyes.

From the hall below came a terrifying banshee howl as Squires released the Alsatian. Donner and Garvald swayed together for a moment and then the dog erupted into the corridor, skidding on its haunches.

With a tremendous heave, Garvald sent Donner staggering along the corridor towards the stair-head. He dropped to one knee, picked up the shotgun and thumbed back the hammer. The dog was already half-way along the corridor when he started to swing the barrel. It leapt forward and he fired, the blast catching it in mid-air.

The Alsatian gave a sort of strangled whimper and fell against the wall where it lay on the floor, kicking feebly. There was a hoarse cry of anger and Squires appeared at the other end of the passage to join Donner, Manton at his shoulder. As all three started forward, Garvald threw the shotgun at them, turned and ran back along the corridor.

A narrow service staircase dropped into darkness and he thundered down it and found himself in a stone-flagged passage at the bottom. He wrenched open the door at the far end and ran into the courtyard.

The light from the kitchen window falling across the cobbles showed him the ten-foot wall on the far side and a narrow door. He wrestled ineffectually for a moment with its rusted bolts, then turned to the place where the stable joined the wall. With the aid of a drain pipe, and using the sill of the stable window as a middle step, he pulled himself on to the sloping roof. He swung across the wall, hung by his hands for a moment and dropped into wet grass.

He got to one knee and an arm slid around his throat, a hand applied pressure savagely. As he moved, the pressure increased, completely cutting off the supply of air to his lungs.

A match flared and Chuck Lazer said: 'Lay off, General. It's Ben.'

*   *   *

Nick released his grip. Garvald stayed on one knee for a moment, shaking his head, a hand at his throat, then he got to his feet. 'Where's your car?'

'At the end of the lane.'

'Then let's get moving.'

Nick grabbed his arm. 'Not so fast, Garvald. We heard what sounded like a shotgun blast inside there a minute or so ago.'

'You're damned right you did. The old sod they have running this dump put his Alsatian on me. I had to finish it off. You going to arrest me for that?'

'Could be. Depends on how you answer my questions. Let's get moving.'

They hurried back along the lane to the main road. The Mini-Cooper was parked under some trees, lights out, and Nick opened the door. 'Get in the back.'

Garvald obeyed without hesitation, his mind working furiously. He had already wasted a great deal of time and things seemed to be getting completely out of hand. Far better to pick up what he had come for and get out of town fast. But first he had to get rid of Miller and from the look of him that wouldn't be easy.

'How did you know where I was?'

The American turned in his seat to face him. 'I remembered you saying you had a room at the Regent Hotel. The Irish bird who does the night

188

shift there filled us in on the rest with a little persuasion.'

'I'd like to fill her in, the bitch.' Garvald lit a cigarette and leaned back. 'What's all this then, Chuck? You playing at being an aide to the CID or something?'

'For God's sake, Ben. I was trying to help you.'

'Sounds pretty thin to me.' Garvald turned to Nick. 'Why the witch hunt? I'm clean as a whistle. Only got into town a few hours ago.'

'When I started looking for you earlier tonight, Garvald, it was only to warn you to stay away from Bella.'

'So she's behind it?' Garvald chuckled. 'She's safe enough, copper. I wouldn't touch her with a ten-foot pole.'

'Then you came back for the money,' Nick said calmly. 'Your share of the take from that Steel Amalgamated job. The best part of eight thousand quid. Nothing else fits.'

Garvald, searching desperately for a way out, played a hunch. 'How's Brady?'

'For Christ's sake, Ben, what do you know about Brady?' Chuck Lazer cried.

Nick cut in, his voice cold and hard. 'What about Brady, Garvald?'

'One of your blokes, isn't he?' Garvald said. 'Turned up at the Flamingo earlier looking for me. There was some kind of a row and Donner knocked him down the stairs of Manton's private entrance.'

'He was found lying in a street near the river,' Nick said. 'Looked like a hit and run.'

'Now I call that neat.' Garvald smiled softly. 'That would be Manton's idea. Takes a fine, twisted mind like his to think up a touch like that.'

'You're sure about this?'

'I saw it happen, I was hiding in a linen cupboard in the same corridor.' Garvald laughed harshly. 'Why in the hell do you think Manton and his boys picked me up at the Regent? They killed a copper and I was the only witness. I can imagine what they intended to do with me.'

'The irony is that Brady isn't dead,' Nick said. 'He's still unconscious, but they think he stands a fair chance of pulling through.'

'And Manton doesn't know that?'

'He does now.' Lazer turned to Nick. 'I was making conversation with him in the kitchen, trying to be natural. I mentioned about Brady being in hospital and so on in passing. Come to think of it, he and Donner both looked pretty sick about it.'

'They'll have to run,' Garvald said calmly. 'No other choice.'

He sat back, well content, and lit a cigarette. The peelers looked after their own. From this moment on, anything else would have to take second place to the Brady affair and they wouldn't rest till they had Manton and his friends with the cuffs on, which caused him no pain at all. Manton was a rat. He'd had something like this coming to him for years.

Nick's problem was a more immediate one. With no radio telephone he was unable to communicate with Headquarters, and without help it would be quite impossible for him to nail Manton and his two tearaways.

The problem solved itself as Manton's Jaguar skidded out of the lane no more than twenty yards away and drove off fast towards town. Nick didn't hesitate. He pressed the starter and the Mini-Cooper shot away, tyres spinning slightly on the wet asphalt.

'You've got a hope.' Garvald laughed.

'You've been out of circulation a long time,' Nick said. 'This is the original wolf in sheep's clothing.'

The Mini-Cooper touched seventy miles an hour in exactly thirty-one seconds and the needle continued to swing, until on the dual carriageway leading to the outer ring road they almost touched ninety.

'God in heaven, what is this thing?' Ben Garvald shouted.

Nick grinned, concentrating all his attention on the lights of the Jaguar in front, gleaming through the heavy rain. 'The greatest invention since the horse.'

As they emerged from the dual carriageway, he braked, then accelerated into a shallow corner and the Mini-Cooper shot round, all four wheels glued to the ground.

The Jaguar was no more than fifty yards ahead now and going well. Garvald leaned over the seat and touched Nick on the shoulder. 'You'll be on your own, have you thought of that, copper? Three to one and Donner's the kind who'd sell his sister if he was short of beer money.'

Nick ignored him, concentrating wholly on the Jaguar, gauging the distance between them, timing his move in advance to the last fraction of a second. He was right on the big car's tail now. Quite suddenly, he dropped into third, pulled out and jammed his foot hard on the accelerator. The Mini-Cooper moved alongside the Jaguar and he took the little car in close and started to brake.

As he swung the wheel, he glanced across. Only one man sat in the other car, the driver, and as he too braked hard, the Jaguar skidded, its nearside wheels cutting into the grass banking at the side of the road. As it came to a halt, Nick pulled in ahead, switched off his own engine and jumped out.

Jango was just a little slower. He scrambled out of the Jaguar and started to run. A hand grabbed him by the shoulder, spun him round and sent him crashing back against the car.

He reacted with the habitual criminal's usual blend of outraged innocence and aggression. 'Hey, what in the hell is this?'

A hand was clamped around his throat so viciously that he cried out in agony and swung wildly at the pale blur of the face in front of him.

For the second time that night a fist lifted into his stomach. As he lay with his face in the wet grass, his arms were jerked behind him, steel bracelets snapped into place with a cold finality and fear moved in his very bowels.

Lazer had got out of the passenger seat and stood beside the open door of the Mini-Cooper staring through the darkness towards the Jaguar. He was aware of a sudden movement inside and turned quickly. Ben Garvald was sliding behind the wheel.

He grinned as he reached for the starter. 'I've got things to do, Chuck. Maybe I'll be seeing you, but it isn't likely. Give Miller my respects. In other circumstances, I'd have enjoyed hating him.'

As the engine roared into life he pushed hard, catching Lazer full in the face, sending him staggering backwards. As the American recovered his balance, the door slammed and the Mini-Cooper faded into the night.

19

It was just after three and for at least twenty or thirty of the guests who refused to go home, the party was still going strong. Harry Faulkner had taken over the barman's duties in the Long Room and half a dozen couples danced to a record player.

Bella had long since reached the stage when the gin was beginning to stick in her throat and all at once a strange thing happened. Every face she looked into seemed weak and evil and selfish and when she turned quickly to a mirror, what she saw there repelled her most of all.

Too much to drink, that's what it was. What she needed was a good soak in a hot tub and about twelve solid hours of sleep. She crossed the hall, went into the library and locked the door.

The bathroom was in black-veined marble and gold, the bath itself half-set into the tiled floor.

She turned on the water, then returned to the bedroom and undressed quickly, throwing her dress and underclothes carelessly on the bed.

She stood in front of the dressing-table mirror for a full minute, examining her magnificent body in detail. The breasts were still high and firm, her flesh unmarked, but there was a perceptible thickening around the waist and the way the skin was starting to bulge beneath her chin boded ill.

She went into the bathroom and stepped down into the hot water, revelling in the sense of physical release it always gave her. She lay there looking up at the ceiling, going over the evening's events in her mind, thinking about Ben. The strange thing was that she could form no clear mental picture of how he looked. Still, it had been a long time. She sat up and reached for the soap and was immediately conscious of a slight draught as if the door was open. When she turned, Ben was standing there smiling down at her.

He stuck a cigarette in his mouth and grinned. 'A long time, angel, but you still look good to me.'

And she wasn't afraid, which was strange because she had thought that she would be. She looked up at him and something stirred in her. A memory of her youth, perhaps, when nothing had ever seemed to matter very much except having a good time. And then Ben had come into her life, this handsome, smiling Irish devil who could put the fear of God in any man who ever crossed him, but who was everything a woman could desire.

She pushed herself up and stood there, the water draining from her breasts, steam curling from her rounded limbs. 'You'd better pass me a towel.'

He was still smiling, the sight of her having no apparent effect. He dropped his cigarette to the floor, pulled a bath towel from the rack and crossed to her. 'What do you want me to do, angel, dry your back?'

'It wouldn't be the first time,' she said calmly.

He draped the towel around her shoulders, then in one quick movement scooped her up into his arms. She could feel the heart move in her, the hollowness in her stomach as she looked up at him and a sudden indolent warmth seeped through her limbs.

She slid her damp arms around his neck, the towel slipping to her waist, her breasts crushed against him, and as he turned and walked into the bedroom, her mouth found his, her tongue working passionately.

She pulled away and rubbed her cheek against his. 'Ben, oh Ben,' she whispered.

'I know, angel, isn't love grand?' He dropped her on the bed and stood back, a grin on his face. 'By God, you must warm the cockles of poor old Harry Faulkner's heart.'

She lay there, raised on one elbow, the towel

covering less than half of her beautiful body and glared up at him, fire in her eyes.

'All right then, what *do* you want?'

'My money, angel, that's all. Seven thousand eight hundred and fifty quid. No fortune, but what my old grannie back in County Antrim would have called a respectable portion. Not much to show for nine years in the nick, but it'll give me a start.'

She lay there staring up at him, a slight fixed frown on her face, and he stopped smiling. 'You've still got it, haven't you?'

She nodded and sat up, pulling the towel around her shoulders. 'Not here though.'

He frowned. 'That's not so good. I was hoping to be out of town by breakfast. I would have thought that would have suited you, too.'

'I've got a motor cruiser moored at Hagen's Wharf on the river,' she said. 'Harry bought it for my birthday last year. The money's there. I'll be glad to see the back of it.'

'That's fine,' Garvald said. 'I've got a car. I'd say it shouldn't take us more than ten minutes to get there from here.'

She got to her feet and stood there, still holding the towel about her. 'If you'd kindly get to hell out of here, I could get dressed. You'll find a drink in the other room.'

'Time was,' he said and started to laugh. He was still laughing when he went into the library.

The moment the door closed, Bella sat on the edge of the bed and reached for the telephone. She dialled a number quickly and the receiver at the other end was lifted almost at once.

'He's here,' she said. 'We'll be leaving in ten minutes.'

The receiver at the other end was replaced immediately and Bella dropped her own into its cradle and dressed quickly in slacks, knee-length Cossack boots and a heavy sheepskin coat. She stood in front of the dressing-table mirror to fasten a silk scarf peasant-fashion around her head.

Last of all, she moved across to a bureau, unlocked a drawer with a small key and took out a Smith & Wesson .38 calibre automatic. For a long moment she looked down at it, gripping the handle so tightly that her knuckles gleamed white to the bone, and then she slipped the gun into her pocket and went into the library.

Bluey Squires sat at the kitchen table and stared vacantly into space, a glass in one hand, a bottle in the other. He was thinking about his dog and he looked across at the bundle in the corner by the fire covered with an old sack.

The strange thing was that he didn't blame Garvald. It was all Manton's fault. Manton and that wall-eyed bastard, Donner. If they hadn't brought

Garvald to The Grange in the first place, the whole damn thing would never have happened.

There was the sound of a car drawing up outside in the yard and he got to his feet, went to the window and peered into the rain. The Jaguar was parked a couple of feet from the front door and he unlocked it quickly.

What happened then was like something out of a strange, distorted dream. The nearside door of the Jaguar opened and a large man moved out with surprising speed, a man with creased, weatherbeaten features which Squires instantly recognized.

He stood there with his mouth open and a hand like a dinner plate wrapped itself around his throat and Grant said softly: 'Where are they, Bluey? I want 'em and I want 'em quick.'

He released his grip and Squires took a great sobbing breath. 'Upstairs, Mr Grant. Manton's got an office on the first floor. It's the only other room in the house that's furnished.'

He moved back as the room seemed to fill with policemen and Grant said, 'Right then, Bluey. If you want to come out of this with a whole skin, this is what you're going to do.'

Manton swallowed his whisky and looked at his watch for the fifth time in as many minutes. 'He's taking his own sweet time.'

Donner laughed harshly. 'Maybe the scuffers have got him.'

He sat on the edge of the desk, the shotgun across his knees, a cigarette smouldering in one corner of his mouth, his good eye half closed, the other fixed, staring unpleasantly. He was more than a little drunk and he reached for the bottle to pour himself another.

'Lay off that stuff,' Manton said angrily. 'You're going to need all your wits about you if we're to see this night through.'

'Your days of telling me what to do are over, Mr Manton,' Donner said, pouring himself another whisky.

Manton took a step towards him and pulled up short as someone knocked on the door. He moved across quickly.

'Who is it?'

'It's me, Mr Manton,' Bluey Squires called. 'Jango's back.'

Manton felt the relief surge through him in a great wave and he turned the key. In the same moment, the door swung in on him. He was aware of Grant with a face like some avenging God and Miller at his side, eyes like dark holes in a bone-white face. And beyond them, the others, big men in blue uniforms surging forward like a tidal wave, pouring over him.

Donner started to swing the shotgun too late.

As it came up, Nick tossed an office stool that deflected the barrel and the weapon discharged harmlessly into the floor. Grant jumped the last ten feet, one great fist connecting solidly high on Donner's right cheekbone.

A moment later, Donner was struggling on the floor beneath the weight of four good men. It took another two to get him down to the van.

20

As they neared the centre of the town, the fog became thicker and Garvald turned the Mini-Cooper off the main road and continued towards the river, keeping to the back streets.

'Where did you get the car?' Bella asked.

'A friend loaned it to me.'

They continued in silence for a little while longer and then she spoke again. 'It's been a long time, hasn't it, Ben? Since we were together like this, I mean.'

'Too long, angel,' he replied and there was a sharp finality in his voice.

She seemed to realize it, took out a gold case and put a cigarette in her mouth. 'What are you going to do next?'

'Once I have the money?' He grinned. 'I'm going home, Bella. Back to the old country. An uncle of mine has a farm in Antrim and no one to follow him. I've had enough of cities.'

She stared at him in genuine astonishment and then started to laugh. 'You, a farmer? I'll believe that when I see it.'

'Stranger things have happened.'

'Name me one.'

'You selling yourself as an old man's bed warmer,' he said with a brutality that stunned her into silence.

As they approached the river, they saw no other traffic and moved into an area of dark canyons flanked by great warehouses shuttered and barred for the night. Garvald braked to a halt at her direction underneath a lamp in a narrow alley beside a gate. Through the iron bars he could see the riding lights of barges moored on the far side of the river glowing through the fog, but the only sound was the lapping of water against the wharf pilings.

'We'll have to walk from here,' she told him.

He got out and moved round to join her. The main gates were locked, but a small judas at one side opened to her touch and they passed through.

One or two ancient gas lamps bracketed to the warehouse walls gave some kind of light, but the fog rolling in from the river reduced visibility considerably.

They passed a door with a sign above it which read *Hagen's Wharf – General Office* and continued across the black shining cobbles to the final lamp at the end of the old warehouse. Beyond that, the railings and wooden planks of the wharf disappeared into the fog and darkness of the river.

'Damn!' Bella said. 'The light's out at the end of the pier. You can't trust these blasted watchmen for more than ten minutes at any one time.'

'Is the boat tied up out there?'

She nodded. 'You wait here. I'll go back to the office for a hand lamp. I've got a key.'

She walked away quietly, the sound of her leather boots on the cobbles dying away almost at once. Garvald took out a cigarette, lit it and stood there staring gloomily into the fog.

By rights, he should have been feeling great because for the first time in his life he was really trying to break out of something. Instead, he felt strangely sad. The lamp above his head, the wharf in front of him stretching into darkness, seemed unreal and transitory as if they might dissolve into the fog at any moment.

The years that the locusts have eaten. As the quotation jumped into his mind, it carried with it a memory of his old grandmother, her Bible on her knee, reading on a Friday night to a boy who still had life ahead of him with all its hopes and dreams and breathless wonderment.

He heard her steps on the cobbles again and started to turn. 'That didn't take long.'

He was aware of only one thing in that final frozen second of life when time seemed to stand still – the muzzle of the gun that was thrust out towards him. Flame exploded in the night and he staggered backwards against the wooden railing of the wharf. He half-turned, clutching at it for support, and as the railing splintered and broke the second bullet caught him in the back and sent him over the edge into an eternal darkness.

21

When Harry Faulkner went into the main CID office at Police Headquarters it was exactly four-fifteen. The first person he saw was Chuck Lazer, who sat at a vacant desk playing Patience, a mug of tea beside him.

'What in the hell are you doing here?' Faulkner demanded in bewilderment.

'I'm what they call an aide to the CID,' Lazer said. 'Fascinating work, but the pay stinks.'

The door to Grant's office opened and a young constable came out. 'In here, Mr Faulkner. Superintendent Grant would like a few words with you.'

Grant was sitting at his desk in his overcoat. Sweat glistened on his forehead and he wiped it away with his sleeve, took a strip of Aspro from his pocket and popped two into his mouth. He swallowed some tea from the pint pot at his elbow and made a face.

'Fill it up with something drinkable, there's a good lad.'

The constable took the pot and retired and Faulkner sat down in the chair on the other side of the desk, a frown on his face.

'And what's all this about then?'

'We've arrested Fred Manton,' Grant said, applying a match to his pipe. 'I thought you'd like to know, you being his employer and so on.'

Faulkner was too old a bird to be drawn. He took a cigarette from his case and lit it with a brass lighter. 'What's the charge?'

'At the moment I'd say attempted murder of a police officer.'

Faulkner's face went grey. 'You know what you're doing?'

'Too bloody right I do,' Grant said. 'If you're interested, he was going to do a bunk with all the ready cash he could lay his hands on. Your money, of course.'

'The bastard,' Faulkner said. 'After all I've done for him.'

'I'm sending a couple of officers to the Flamingo now,' Grant said. 'They'll have a warrant empowering them to make a thorough search of Manton's office and apartment. I think you should be there as owner, just to confirm that everything's in order. I'd particularly like to see an inventory of the contents of the safe.'

'Anything to help,' Faulkner said calmly. 'You know me.'

'Somehow that's what I thought you'd say. You'll find Detective Constable Carter and a uniformed officer waiting for you downstairs.'

Faulkner moved to the door, opened it and stood back as the young constable entered with Grant's tea. 'Just one more thing, Mr Faulkner,' Grant said. 'If you could return here with the two officers when the search has been completed. I'd like a general statement from you concerning Manton.'

'Is that really necessary?'

'I'd appreciate any help you can give me. Any help at all.'

Faulkner looked at him, a slight frown on his face as if he couldn't quite understand which way things were going and then he shrugged.

'See you later, then.'

The door closed behind him and Grant reached for the pot of tea and carried it to his lips. He made a face and hurriedly put the pot down again.

'It's freshly made, sir,' the young constable said defensively.

'It's not your fault, lad,' Grant said. 'It's me. I'm getting too damned old for this game. I last saw a bed twenty hours ago, I've a temperature of 102 and my mouth tastes like a Russian wrestler's armpit.'

'Is there anything I can do, sir?'

'Yes, find yourself a decent job while you're still young enough to get out.' Grant got to his feet, moved to the door, opened it and turned. 'If you quote me on that, I'll have you skinned.'

As he moved through the outer office, Lazer looked up and shook his head. 'You look like something the tomb just threw up.'

'Nothing to how I feel.'

Grant walked along the corridor, opened the door of the Interrogation Room and went in. Manton sat at the table in the centre, his head in his hands. The uniformed constable in the chair by the door got to his feet. Grant nodded, moved across to the table, sat in the chair opposite Manton and lit a cigarette.

Rain drummed against the window and the grey-green walls seemed to swim out of the shadows. There was a smell of stale cigarette smoke and fog, sharp and acrid. Manton's head was aching and when he touched the side of his face, there was a three-inch split in the skin, swollen and tender where someone's fist had landed during the fight at The Grange.

'All right, we'll try again.' Grant's voice seemed to come from deep under the sea. 'From the beginning.'

'I want a lawyer,' Manton said in a washed-out voice. 'I know my rights.'

'You're going to need one before I'm through with you,' Grant said. 'Now let's have it.'

'All right, damn you. For the third time, it was Ben Garvald. He was upstairs at the club visiting me when Brady arrived. Garvald wanted to get away and Brady tried to stop him. It was as simple as that.'

'So Garvald tossed him downstairs?'

'They were fighting. I don't think Ben meant to play it that way. It just happened.'

'And what a sweet touch that remark is. They broke the mould the day they made you.'

'That's my story and I'm sticking to it,' Manton said stubbornly.

'Until Jack Brady regains consciousness. What happens if he tells us something different?'

'Maybe he won't come round. He fell a long way.'

'Tell me again what happened after the fall. I like that bit.'

'Garvald had a car parked round the back. He thought Brady was dead so he carted him away over his shoulder. Said he was going to dump him somewhere and make the whole thing look like an accident.'

'And you and Donner and Stavrou just stood around and watched?'

'Garvald told us to stay out of it. He said he might just as easily swing for two as one.'

'Which frightened you all to death, I'm sure.'

The door opened and Nick entered. 'How's he doing? Still the same yarn?'

'Word for word. He and Donner must have been doing their homework together.'

Nick handed him a foolscap form without a word. Grant read it quickly and started to laugh. 'This is fine by me. Let our friend here see it, then take him downstairs and book him.'

He slapped the form down on the table and walked out without a word to Manton who picked it up with shaking hands, a frown on his face.

City Police
PRISONER'S VOLUNTARY STATEMENT

In all cases where a prisoner is arrested on a charge of felony, or other serious charge, the Officer arresting should at once, when charging him, warn him that he is not obliged to say anything, but that anything he may say may be taken down in writing and used in evidence. Having administered this caution, the Officer will write on this form as nearly as possible, word for word, any statement bearing on the charge which the prisoner may make. This statement must then be forwarded through the Superintendent of the Division to the Chief Constable to be retained by him until the trial of the prisoner . . .

My name is Alexias Stavrou, known to my friends as Jango Stavrou, and I am employed as assistant manager at the Flamingo Club in Gascoigne Square. I was near the staff entrance just after midnight when Mr Brady comes in and says he wants Ben Garvald. I told him I didn't even know who Garvald was, not knowing then that he was upstairs with Mr Manton. Frank Donner arrived and there was more argument. Mr Brady forced his way upstairs, but Garvald had gone so he started to search the rooms. Donner told Mr Manton to give him a couple of fivers to get rid of him. Mr Brady got very angry. There was an argument. Donner kicked him in the crutch and Mr Brady fell down the stairs to the private entrance. Garvald then came out of the linen cupboard where he'd been hiding. He left by the side door and Mr Manton told me to go after him. I followed Garvald to the Regent Hotel in Gloyne Street. When I went back, I found Mr Manton hiding in Stank's Yard near the club. He told me that Brady was dead and that Donner had gone to lift a van. They were going to dump Mr Brady in a street somewhere and make it look like a hit-and-run accident. I told Mr Manton I didn't want to be mixed up in it, but he threatened me. He knows I was a member of EOKA for five years during the troubles in Cyprus and that I am in this country on a false passport. We left Mr Brady in a street near the river after making it look like an accident. Donner wanted to run over him with the van just to make it look good, but another car came and we had to leave. Donner dumped the van off Grainger's Wharf. Afterwards, on Mr Manton's orders, we picked up Garvald at the Regent Hotel and took him to The Grange at Ryescroft, because he was a witness to what had happened, but he got away. Mr Manton told me to take his Jaguar and go to the Flamingo and bring him what was in the safe. He said his boss, Mr Faulkner, had been on the phone and needed ready cash because of a run on the house at one of his gambling clubs. On my way to the club I was arrested by Mr Miller who told me the true facts and how Mr Brady wasn't dead after all. That's all I got to say and it's the truth, I swear this on my mother's grave.

SIGNED: Alexias Stavrou

Manton sat staring at the statement for a long moment after he had finished it. Nick reached over and took it from his hands.

'Anything to say?'

'If you can make it stick, if you can't . . .

Manton helped himself to a cigarette from the packet on the table and Nick gave him a light. 'Fair enough, Manton. There's just one more thing. What about Garvald? Why did he come back? Is the cash from that Steel Amalgamated job still lying around somewhere?'

'Why should I make it easy for you bastards, they're paying you enough, aren't they?' Manton pushed back his chair. 'Take me downstairs and let's get it over with. I could do with some sleep.'

'You'll have plenty of time for that where you're going. There isn't much else to do.'

As they turned to the door, it opened and Grant entered. His face was hard and set, the lines scoured deep. He nodded to the constable. 'Take him down, will you? I'd like a word with Sergeant Miller.'

The door closed behind them and Nick shook his head. 'He'll hang on to that lie until he sees whether Jack Brady pulls through or not. Understandable, I suppose. He's got nothing to lose now.'

'They've found your car,' Grant said.

'Where?'

'Hagen's Wharf on the river. Parked just up the street from the entrance. The gate was open so the beat man thought he'd have a look round in case Garvald was there.'

'And was he?'

Grant nodded. 'He's lying on a mudbank at the far end of the wharf. From the sound of it, he's been shot to death.'

22

The big black van that was known throughout the Department as the Studio was already parked by the pier at the end of Hagen's Wharf when Nick and Grant arrived.

A couple of constables were rigging an arc lamp powered by the van's emergency lighting system under the supervision of Henry Wade, the Detective Sergeant in charge of the Studio.

Wade was a large, fat man with several chins and horn-rimmed spectacles that made him look deceptively benign. He wore a heavy overcoat and Homburg hat and looked like a prosperous back-street bookie. When he moved, he moved slowly, but in his line of country, only brains counted and those he had to a remarkable degree.

'Quick work, Henry,' Grant said as they approached.

'Makes a change to get something interesting,'

Wade replied. 'We were at a break-in at Parson's Foundry when I got the call.' He looked at Nick curiously. 'Who's this, the college boy?'

Nick ignored him and moved past the van to the end of the pier as someone switched on the arc lamp and light flooded down across the splintered rail.

Ben Garvald lay on his back in the mud, one leg twisted underneath him, right arm outstretched, fingers curling slightly. The eyes were wide open, fixed on a point in eternity a million light years away, and there was a slight, bewildered smile on his mouth as if he couldn't quite believe in what was happening to him. It was almost as if he might scramble to his feet at any moment, but that wasn't possible because of the ragged hole in the neck just beneath his chin and the bloodsoaked rent in his raincoat below the left breast where the second bullet had emerged.

Nick stared down at the body, hands in pockets, dark eyes brooding in the white face. Six or seven hours since he'd heard Ben Garvald's name for the first time. Since then, a composite picture of the man had emerged from records, at first shadowy and insubstantial, flesh growing on the bones as people who had known him had their say and finally, ten minutes' conversation face to face.

And in the end, he'd known Ben Garvald better than any of them. Did this explain the strange sense of personal loss he now felt as he looked down at the body below?

'He doesn't look too good, does he?' Grant commented.

Nick shook his head. 'I don't know what happened, but he deserved better than this.'

Grant stared at him curiously, then turned to Wade who was pulling on a pair of gumboots. 'Going down now, Henry?'

'In a minute. You want the lot, do you?'

'Every damn thing in the book. Casts of any foot-prints, just in case the killer went down to make sure he was dead, and photograph everything in sight. And don't forget Miller's car.' He turned to Nick. 'Sorry about that, but you'll have to leave it.'

As Wade went over the edge of the pier to the mudbank, Grant beckoned to the young constable who had been standing patiently by the van, his cap streaming with the heavy rain.

'Johnson, sir, 802. Central Division.'

'You're the lad who found him, eh?'

'That's right, sir.'

'Let's have it then.'

'I got the nod about Detective Sergeant Miller's car when I made a point with my sergeant at three-thirty, sir. It was exactly four-fifteen when I came across it.'

'Did you examine it at all?'

'Only to try the doors, sir. They were locked.'

'So you decided to have a look inside?'

'It seemed the logical place and the judas gate was unlocked. I thought whoever it was might still be around so I took a walk along the wharf and checked the doors. I was just going to turn back when my torch picked out the smashed railing.'

Grant glanced at the mud encrusted leggings. 'I see you went down to him.'

'With his eyes open like that I wasn't sure whether he was alive or dead at first. I pulled his wallet out and found his discharge papers and so on. That told me who he was. I made straight for the nearest telephone and reported. Then I came back and waited.'

Which must have taken nerve, Grant reflected, thinking of the fog and the darkness and what lay in the mud below the pier. 'Ever done any aides to CID work, lad?'

'No, sir.'

'We'll have to see what we can do then, won't we? Hang on here until I tell you to go. I might need you later on and there should be a cup of tea going in a minute or two if I know the Studio bunch.'

Johnson tried hard to conceal his pleasure and failed. At that moment, Henry Wade, who had been crouching beside Garvald's body, looked up, the light from the arc lamp glinting on his spectacles.

'I'll tell you one thing, sir. He hasn't been here long.'

Grant turned to Nick. 'He couldn't have been, could he? When was it he took off in your car?'

'About three o'clock.'

'Let's assume he'd been dead for at least half an hour when Johnson found him. That leaves about forty-five minutes to fill. I wonder what he was doing?'

'He only had one purpose in coming back,' Nick said. 'I'm sure of that now.'

'The cash from the Steel Amalgamated job? You still believe in that?'

'More than ever.'

Grant leaned against the van and took the cigarette Nick offered. 'Let's assume you're right. If that cash existed, who would Garvald have left it with? His driver, the man we couldn't catch? If Manton was the wheelman on that job, it would give us another motive for some of the things that have happened tonight.'

Nick shook his head. 'Ben wrote to Bella from prison just before he got out. He said, "See you soon – Ben." Why? He didn't love her any more. He told me himself he wouldn't have touched her with a ten-foot pole and I believed him.'

'Which means he wanted to see her for only one reason?'

'To recover the money she'd been looking after for him all these years. The only weakness I can see in the argument is Bella herself. Knowing her, I would have thought she would have spent it long ago.'

'Not a chance,' Grant said. 'I kept tabs on her for at least a year after Ben went down the steps, just in case she started spending heavily and proved us wrong about that cash going up in flames. She never did. Worked as a waitress for most of the time, then got a job at one of Harry's clubs. From then on she was in clover. He chased her for long enough, believe me, and she made him pay for the privilege.'

A car drew up behind them and a tall, ascetic-looking man in a dark overcoat, a University scarf wrapped around his neck, got out. He carried an old black bag in one hand and nodded to Grant in a familiar manner.

'Can't they pick a more convenient time, for God's sake?'

'Sorry, Professor,' Grant said. 'You'll need gumboots for this one. They'll let you have a pair inside.'

The Professor leaned over the rail and shuddered. 'I see what you mean.'

He put down his bag and turned to the van

and Grant took Nick by the arm and led him a few paces away. 'I've been thinking. By a stroke of luck, Harry Faulkner can only be in one of two places. At the Flamingo or back at Headquarters waiting to see me about the Brady affair. That leaves Bella on her own. It might be an idea if you paid her a visit.'

'What line shall I take?'

'You can start by saying we need her to identify Garvald's body. As his ex-wife she's the nearest thing to next of kin he's got.'

'The news could hit her pretty hard. I got the impression she still had a soft spot for him.'

'That's what I'm counting on. See what her reaction is. If she breaks down, get to work on her straight away while the going's good. No telling what you might come up with. You can take my car. If anything unusual happens, let me know by radio.'

He turned as the Professor emerged from the van in a pair of gumboots a size too large and Nick moved away quickly, glad to be going. At least this gave him something concrete to do that might conceivably lead somewhere.

Grant's car was parked outside the gate in the alley and the driver sat behind the wheel smoking a cigarette. 'The Superintendent's staying here,' Nick told him. 'You can run me up to Harry Faulkner's place in St Martin's Wood.'

He reached for the door handle and the driver said: 'What about the Yank, Sergeant? He's been walking up and down the alley like a cat on hot bricks since you went in.'

Chuck Lazer moved out of the shadows into the light of the solitary lamp above the gate. He looked like a dead man walking, the skin stretched tightly over the emaciated face, the dark fringe beard accentuating the sallowness of his skin.

His eyes asked the question and Nick gave him the answer. 'It's Ben I'm afraid. Shot twice at close quarters from the look of it. Do you want to go in?'

The shock was obviously very great and something seemed to go out of Lazer in a long sigh. He shook his head. 'What would be the point?'

'Can I give you a lift?'

'Where to?' Lazer shook his head. 'He was a nice guy. Too nice to go out this way.'

He turned to walk away and Nick said urgently: 'Chuck, you wouldn't do anything silly, would you?'

Lazer shrugged. 'Does it matter, General? Does anything really matter in this lousy world?'

'We'll find who did it. We'll run them down.'

'So what? It won't bring Ben back. Christ Jesus, General, don't you ever stop to ask yourself what it's all supposed to be about?'

He started to walk away and Nick went after him quickly, catching his arm. 'I'm going up to see Bella, Chuck. We'll need her for the official identification. Come with me. You can stay in the car if you like.'

'What's the angle?'

'Let's just say one good man gone is enough for one night. I probably couldn't take another.'

Lazer stared at him sombrely for several moments without speaking, and then nodded twice as if understanding. Together, they walked back to the car.

23

The house in St Martin's Wood was still ablaze with lights as they drove up, but only four cars were parked in the drive. Music from the record player still sounded faintly through the curtained windows of the Long Room and Nick turned to Lazer.

'Want to come in with me? Sounds as if the party's still going strong.'

'Why not? Maybe they could do with a good piano man.'

They went up the steps together. The door was locked and Nick pressed the bell button hard, keeping his thumb in place for a good half minute.

When the door finally opened, Craig stared out. The side of his face was swollen and angry looking, a purpling bruise already in evidence. From the look of his eyes he had been drinking and he glared.

'What in the hell do you want? The party's over.'

'Doesn't sound that way to me.'

Nick pushed him back with a good stiff arm and walked inside. The hall was empty, but in the Long Room two couples still circled the floor aimlessly and a man in a dinner jacket slept on a Regency divan near the fireplace.

Lazer walked down the room to the record player, turned it off, sat at the piano and started to play. Craig slammed the front door, grabbed Nick by the arm and jerked him round.

Nick pulled himself free with no difficulty. 'Do that again and I'll put you through the wall. Where's Mrs Faulkner?'

'Got a warrant?'

'As it happens I don't need one. Now where is she?'

'I saw her going to her room about half an hour ago. I think she'd had enough.'

'Go and dig her out. Tell her I want a word with her.'

Craig opened his mouth to give an angry reply, but obviously thought better of it. He moved away along the hall and Nick walked down to the piano.

Lazer grinned tiredly. 'We've been here before, General.'

'A long night, Chuck. A hell of a long night,' Nick said. 'How about a drink?'

'I could certainly use one.'

Nick went behind the bar, found a couple of clean glasses and a bottle of Scotch and went back to the piano. He gave Lazer a generous measure, filled his own glass to the brim and took it down in one easy swallow.

'Careful, General, that way it can get to be a habit,' Lazer said.

As the warm glow spread throughout his entire body, Nick poured himself another, then leaned against the piano, the music reaching out to enfold him. It was five o'clock in the morning at the fag end of a long night and he was tired. Too tired to think straight and that wouldn't do, because somewhere, just below the level of consciousness, something was nagging away at him, one piece of the jigsaw that was the key to this whole business and he was damned if he could think what it was.

Craig appeared at his elbow and bowed ironically. 'She isn't feeling too well. You'll have to wait till tomorrow, copper.'

'Tomorrow's already here.' Nick shook his head. 'You want to get with it, Craig. You're slipping.'

He walked down the room, disregarding Craig's sudden cry and moved along the hall to the library. As he opened the door to go in, Craig caught up with him and grabbed at his shoulder. Nick sent him staggering back across the hall, slammed the door and locked it.

The fire in the grate had burned low, but the

lamp was still lit on the desk. He moved across to the bedroom door and knocked. There was no reply and when he tried to open the door, he found it was locked.

He knocked again. 'Bella, this is Nick Miller. I've got to speak to you.'

There was silence for a moment, then a soft foot-fall, the click of a key. When he opened the door, she was moving across to the fireplace.

She wore a négligé of black silk, the sleeves trimmed with mink and her face was very pale, the eyes like dark shadows. She picked up a glass from the side table, poured a double gin and turned to face him, curiously defiant.

'What's Harry been up to then? Don't tell me you've managed to pin something on him after all these years?'

'Harry?' Nick frowned and then he remembered. 'You've got it all wrong, Bella. Fred Manton's the one who's gone in too deep. He was going to make a run for it with the contents of the safe at the Flamingo. Harry was invited down to check on things, that's all.'

A stranger stared out from the mirror behind her. A man in a blue raincoat whose dark eyes beneath the peak of the semi-military cap stared through and beyond.

She shivered and swallowed some of her gin hurriedly. 'Is that all you wanted to say?'

'No, I came to tell you that Ben won't bother you any more.'

There was something in her eyes, but only for a moment and her head went back. 'Is that a fact? Well you can tell him to go to hell as far as I'm concerned.'

'He wouldn't hear me,' Nick said calmly. 'He's lying on his back in the mud at the end of Hagen's Wharf, Bella. Somebody put a couple of bullets in him.'

Until then it had been only a nightmare compounded of the rain and the fog and the night, something to be shrugged off in the light of morning, to be forgotten as quickly as any bad dream.

But now, in one terrible visionary moment of clarity she saw him lying there in the mud, the smile hooked into place, and it was only then that the full force of what had happened hit her.

She dropped the glass and put out a hand as if to ward him off and her head turned from side to side, her face contorting until the vomit rose in her throat and she staggered across to the bathroom, a hand to her mouth.

She leaned over the sink, her shoulders heaving, and Nick stood in the door and watched her, strangely calm. It was as if he stood outside himself, outside of both of them, but that was the whisky talking. He stood in the shadows of the other room looking in at himself and this woman and knew with the most tremendous certainty that he was standing right on the brink of something.

He caught her by the shoulder and jerked her round. 'Why did Ben come back in the first place, Bella? It was to pick up the money, wasn't it? The money you've been keeping for him all these years. His share of the Steel Amalgamated hoist?'

She pushed him hard against the wall and staggered into the other room. 'Get out!' she screamed. 'Go on, get out!'

'He was here tonight, wasn't he?'

'No, it isn't true. I haven't seen Ben Garvald in nine years.'

She tried to rush past him, he grabbed her by the arm and swung her back across the bed. She lay there staring up at him, terror in her eyes, and he leaned over her.

'He told me he wouldn't touch you with a ten-foot pole and I believed him, so why else would he want to see you? It had to be the money.'

He reached into his inside breast pocket and pulled out his wallet and various papers, scattering them on the bed, searching through them with one hand while he held her wrist with the other.

He found the letter, opened it quickly, and held it in front of her. 'He wrote from prison warning you he was coming, didn't he? There's his letter.'

Her face shattered like a mirror breaking. He

released his grip on her wrist and looked at the letter, a frown on his face, and what he saw there hit him low down in the stomach like a kick from a mule.

As she started to sob hysterically, he grabbed her by the throat and forced back her head. 'Right, you bitch, and now we'll have the truth.'

24

It was almost 6 A.M. when Jean Fleming opened the side gate and went into the school yard. In the grey light of early morning, the fog had receded, but rain still hammered down as relentlessly as ever, drifting in a curtain before the wind.

She ran into the porch, searching for her key with one hand, a carton of milk in the other and a newspaper tucked under one arm. She finally got the door open and paused, a slight frown on her face. Someone was playing the piano in the music room.

Nick was tired, more tired than he had ever known. It had been a long night and now the Graveyard Shift was ending. He glanced up as Jean opened the door. She placed the carton of milk and the newspaper on top of a desk, untied the damp scarf which had covered her head and ran her fingers through her dark hair as she came forward.

She was wearing her heavy sheepskin coat, Cossack boots and a hand-tailored tweed skirt, and stood so close that he only had to reach out to touch her. He wondered whether this ever happened more than once in a lifetime? This strange blend of love and desire and the flesh that was almost physical in its pain.

'You look beautiful,' he said, continuing to play. 'More beautiful than I ever believed a woman could look at this hour in the morning. Did you manage to get some sleep?'

'Not really. I was waiting for you.'

'But I told you I wouldn't be able to make it before the end of my shift.'

'Are you finished now?'

He looked up at the clock on the wall. 'Not quite. Ten minutes to go.'

She smiled. 'You've come to have breakfast with me?'

He shook his head. 'No, Jean, I've come to take you downtown.'

'Downtown?' The smile was still there, but the eyes had frozen hard. 'To Police Headquarters you mean?'

'That's right. I'm arresting you for the murder of Ben Garvald.'

And she didn't try to deny it, that was the

strange thing. She stood there looking at him, somehow completely detached, outside of all this, the sallow peasant face quite composed.

Nick stopped playing. He took a packet of cigarettes from his pocket, pushed one in his mouth and searched for matches. He found them, lit his cigarette and coughed as smoke caught at the back of his throat.

'May I have one?'

He pushed the packet along the top of the piano and gave her a light. She inhaled deeply and looked down at him, quite calm.

'Hadn't you better get on with it?'

'All right.' He started to play again, his hands moving slowly over the keys, a progression of quiet, sad chords that were autumn and winter rolled into one. 'One or two things about this business had been nagging away at me all night. The letter, for example. The one Ben was supposed to have sent to Bella.'

'Supposed?'

'He had to go and see Chuck Lazer to find out who she'd married, never mind where she lived. How in the hell could he have written to her? I suppose you helped yourself to a little prison notepaper when you last saw him? Easy enough. There's always a supply on hand in the Visiting Room.'

'You'd have difficulty in proving that.'

'I don't think so.'

He took a folded sheet of blue notepaper from his wallet and laid it down on top of the piano. Printed at the top was the legend:

In replying to this letter, please write on the envelope:
Number ....
Name ....
....Prison

This side of the sheet was blank. When he turned it over, Jean Fleming's name and telephone number were written on the other side in her own hand. He produced Ben's letter written on the same note-paper and placed it beside the other.

Jean sighed. 'That *was* rather careless of me.'

It was the ease with which she accepted it, her ice-cold calm that horrified him. 'This is all pretty circumstantial, Nick. I'd need a reason.'

'You had one. Ben had to be stopped from ever returning here because once he found there was no money waiting for him, you couldn't be sure how he would react. You checked on his release date, then forged the letter.'

'To frighten Bella?'

'Only partly. You wanted something to show Harry Faulkner. You knew he'd arrange things. A show of force, perhaps, that would frighten Ben away. You made a mistake there. Ben Garvald wasn't the sort of man to be frightened by anything. You came to us just to make it look good.'

'You've been to Bella.'

He nodded. 'Once I told her how much I'd worked out for myself, she soon came across with the rest. She even told me about the divorce. How Ben suggested she go through with it as a blind to allay any possible suspicion by the police that she just might have that money.'

'Did she tell you she was Ben's driver when he pulled the Steel Amalgamated job?'

'You were her alibi. You swore to the police that she hadn't been out of the house all night and, afterwards, blackmailed her. You put the screws on your own sister. She knew that all you had to do was open your mouth and she'd get five years.'

'I needed that money,' she said calmly.

'I realize that now,' he said. 'Four years at University. Did you really work as a barmaid at nights, by the way? And then there was this place. You said you were paying Miss Van Heflin a percentage of your profits each year. You didn't tell me you gave her a down payment of three thousand pounds. She did. I hauled her out of bed and spoke to her on the phone half an hour ago. A nice old girl. She hopes you haven't done anything wrong, by the way.'

Her iron composure cracked and she slammed a fist down hard on top of the piano. 'I had to get out of Khyber Street, Nick. You can understand that? I had to.'

'And what about Ben?'

'He was going to spoil everything. If he'd had some sense, if he'd stayed away, none of this would have happened.'

'Bella told me how you arranged things. That if Ben turned up she was to give him a phoney story about the money being hidden on board a boat she was supposed to have moored at Hagen's Wharf. You asked her to bring the gun for protection only. You were going to bribe Ben to go away. That's what you told her.'

Jean shrugged. 'Poor Bella, she could never really handle anything when the going got rough. I had to do it all for her, even when I was a kid. You'll never find the gun, you know.'

'That doesn't matter. We'll run a nitrate test on your hands. That'll show whether you've fired a gun recently. And the mud on that wharf – a lab analysis of the dirt on your boots should tie in pretty closely. Then there's your car. If it was parked for long in the alley outside the wharf, we can prove that, too.' He shook his head. 'You never stood a chance.'

'Didn't I?'

'You know what your biggest mistake was? You

told me you hated Ben, that from the age of fourteen on, he wouldn't leave you alone.' Nick shook his head. 'If there was one thing I learned during the past eight hours, it was this. Where women were concerned, Ben Garvald was the original gentleman. He'd have cut off his right hand before he'd have harmed a fourteen-year-old kid.'

'I wanted him,' Jean said simply. 'Do you know that? I used to lie in bed nights and burn for him and he never laid a finger on me.'

He got to his feet, dropping his cigarette to the floor, and she moved in close, hands sliding around his neck, breasts pushing hard against him.

'Nobody needs to know, Nick. You could handle it somehow, I know you could.'

'If I wanted to,' he said slowly. 'And there's the rub. To use the words of a man who was worth a dozen of you any day, I wouldn't touch you with a ten-foot barge pole, angel.'

She cracked completely, fingers hooked, clawing at his eyes. As he grabbed her wrists, the language came bursting out like a dam overflowing. All the filth of Khyber Street, the gutter years, pushed down, hidden away in some dark corner of the mind, now rising to the surface.

Grant came through the door, moving with incredible speed for a man of his weight, a constable at his shoulder. He caught her wrists, pulling her away. 'All right, lad, I'll take her.'

The constable took her other arm and she went through the door between them, looking over her shoulder, face twisted with hate, the stream of filth never ending, fading across the yard into the rain.

He stood staring into space, feeling for a cigarette mechanically. He placed it in his mouth and a match flared. He turned, looked into the dark, tortured face of Chuck Lazer for a moment, then leaned to the light.

'A long night, General.'

Nick didn't reply. He walked out of the room, passed along the corridor and stood in the porch, staring out at the driving rain.

'A long night,' he repeated slowly.

'Look, I know how you feel,' Chuck Lazer said awkwardly. 'But she's a woman after all. They'll go easy on her.'

'Go easy on her?' Nick turned, eyes burning in the white face and all the anger, the self-loathing, the frustrated passion seemed to erupt from his mouth in a single sentence.

'God damn her, I hope they hang the bitch.'